LORKDAN

THE LOST CHAPTERS

AJ Cooper

Lorkdan: The Lost Chapters

Copyright © 2021 Andrew James Cooper

Published by Realms of Varda

www.vardabooks.com

Front cover art © Marin Iurii | Dreamstime.com

Back cover art © Pavlo Vakhrushev | Dreamstime.com

ISBN 978-1-958724-20-0

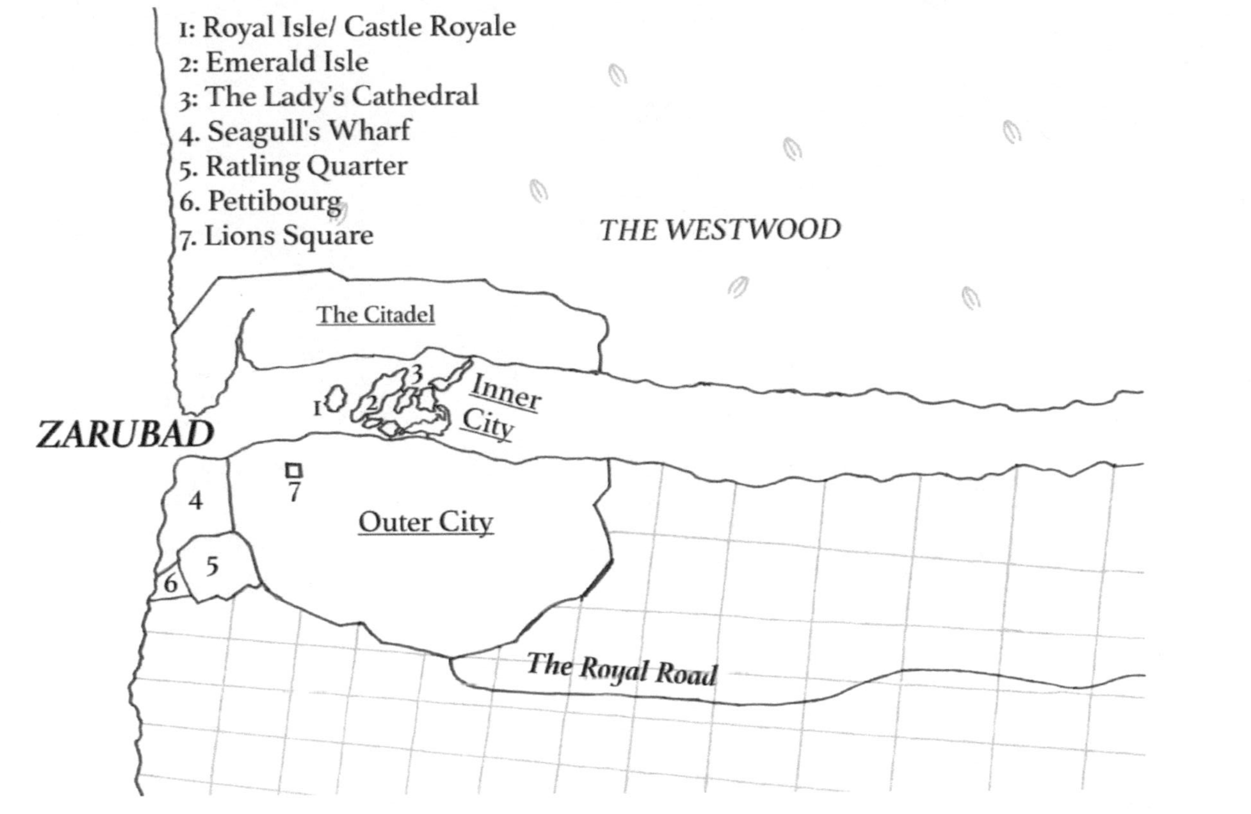

ZARUBAD
1: Royal Isle/ Castle Royale
2: Emerald Isle
3: The Lady's Cathedral
4. Seagull's Wharf
5. Ratling Quarter
6. Pettibourg
7. Lions Square
THE WESTWOOD
The Citadel
Inner City
Outer City
The Royal Road

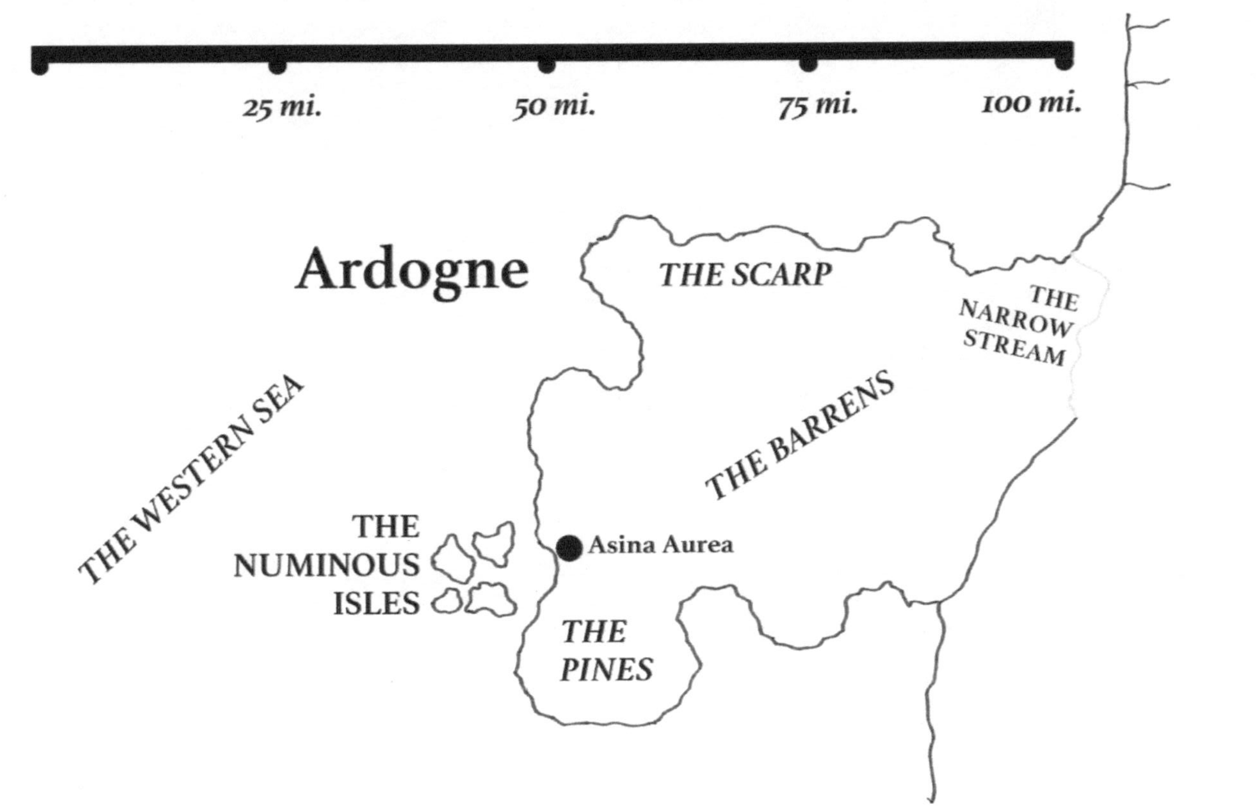

25 mi.
50 mi.
75 mi.
100 mi.
Ardogne
THE SCARP
THE NARROW STREAM
THE WESTERN SEA
THE BARRENS
THE NUMINOUS ISLES
Asina Aurea
THE PINES

Part One

When the war began, I was like a boy, naïve to the world's workings, aimless, adrift.

I was in Zarubad when the war started, at an inn called The Belled Dancer. I was in the Royal City when my journey first began.

—Lorkdan, "Records from Evre Prison"

Chapter One: Nothing Free

For hours, the music had raged, the pipes, the bells, the drums. In a seat, besotted, I sat, with a tall mug of ale, as girls in billowing gowns hopped from table to table and the rabble of the Royal City sang their drinking songs and chansons, "Oomya-ya, Oomya-ya."

I had been a patron of The Belled Dancer so long, that at night, I would often forget why I had come here, why I was in the Royal City in the first place. I would forget I was a mercenary, a hired sword... here because of a promise, here because the king had conscripted me into his service. War was beginning, yes, war, for in the south a deadly foe had appeared, one who would challenge the kingdoms of the north. It was called plainly the Empire, and storm clouds were gathering, and the strength of the Kingdom of Zarubain, for which I would fight, was beginning to seem faint.

I was here... I was promised money. But that money had not yet come.

I was promised money, a task, a way to use my sword, but that call had not arrived, and the armies had not assembled. I was living off a promise, a promise and what coin I had brought with me, and off the kindness of strangers.

I, Lorkdan, called the underworld's champion, was a prideful man, but without charity and a good word from the master of The Belled Dancer, I would be out on the streets with the vagrants and the hoodlums and the urban poor. I would be one of the rabble, and I wouldn't be slaking my thirst on this bubbling ale. My stomach would not be filled with roast pig and crispy bread, and I would not be having a gawk at the lovely women of the Royal City, dancing on a stage and hopping from table to table as they sang their chanson.

I was growing delirious. The ale was sparkling in my glass. It was late at night, past ten hours afternoon. But the Royal City did not sleep, and in taverns and in public houses, there was always life; there were always people hurrying to and fro.

As a man of war, well hewn, with a scar across my cheek and one across the arm, I had no trouble attracting the fine ladies in establishments such as these. But I knew that they of the Royal City, unlike in the East, were most often false and not to be trusted. Love they did not care for; some were after money. They were beautiful and they were free, but as I stared at the dancers, sipping at my glass, I cautioned myself not to fall into their trap. I remembered why I was here.

I had no love for the Kingdom of Zarubain, the nation for which I would supposedly fight. I had no love for the west, where I now dwelled. No, I, a sell-sword, was after one thing, and that thing sparkled in the light of candles, and it made my coin purse fat.

"Lorkdan!" called a voice I knew. It was Esmée, the chief of the serving girls. "Another round?"

And I cautioned myself, for I knew the more tall ales I drank the likelier I would have another, until at last the good kind folk at The Belled Dancer would kick me out, and I'd awaken sickened in a pile of my own filth in some gutter. And that was no way for a sell-sword to be found, no way for a professional to be seen. And I was a professional in a profession that was needed, one that would grow more needed as the war raged on.

"No," I said to Esmée, and her green eyes sparkled, and her winsome little mouth curled up into just the slightest hint of a smile. "No, I…"

But she was taking her platter away, her platter of towering mugs, in which there was a little more liquid gold, a little more sparkling *aqua vita* to whet my appetite.

"Oh, why not," I said.

"Another," I told her, "and likely another after that."

"I thought so," Esmée said, and she sauntered over, grabbing my empty glass, and placing a new one in its stead.

I took the glass in my hand as Esmée wandered off.

The night was growing late, but the crowds in The Belled Dancer were not diminishing; no, they were growing. The Royal City, which never slept, had no end to its entertainments, its opportunities for the indulgement of vice.

And I to my surprise was growing tired. I had a cot in the rafters of The Belled Dancer, which I was provided for free. "Thank you," the master of this public house had said, "for fighting for our country."

A strange thing, it was, to be provided with something for free. A strange thing it was, yes—indeed.

The music was growing louder, the crowds swarming about me. Sometime between my fifth or sixth drink, a serving girl came by and demanded I drink water. I told her I was called the underworld's champion for a reason, and she backed off.

Sometime between drink six and drink seven, a serving girl came by and demanded I leave, and so angry was I, I touched her just slightly, and that was when the storm came, a storm of anger, of volatility. Shouts, faces, glaring eyes—two brawny men with clubs, and I was grabbed by both arms against my protests, and dragged out of my seat. Giggles greeted me, and laughter, and within moments I'd been carried to the threshold of the door. I was tossed unceremoniously into the cold night air, to shouts of, "Lorkdan, underworld's champion, never come to this public house again."

~

I was in the dark, scrambling, and my toes and fingers were

numb. A wind was gently blowing, and the smell of the city was about me. Numb I was, and the liquid gold was in my bloodstream. I needed to relieve myself, but where?

"Look out, water!" someone cried far above me, and from a window of the public house the remnants of a chamber pot were emptied just inches from my feet.

Putrescence, and now I was alone, wandering the street. Putrescence, and now I had nowhere to rest my head.

In the moonlight, I stood, and the city scene that greeted my eyes brought home the squalor of the Royal City. Just a step outside The Belled Dancer was this—the stinking streets, partly of dirt and partly of cobblestone, piles of discarded trash, overturned carts, vagrants on street corners, prostitutes with painted faces wandering about, offering a night of pleasure at the cost of one's long-term health. I knew better than to accept the service of a prostitute whose face was painted. I knew better... but my mind was swimming, and I was not entirely in control of my faculties. I was not entirely well.

And I knew that soon I would be hungry. There was no place to rest my head.

My sword was at my side—I did not fear thugs and hoodlums. Worse I feared... the open air.

When would the king pay me? When would my coin purse be filled?

I had worse things to worry about. Not all was well, not all was well.

I felt myself leaning to the side, ready to tip over, ready to fall. And in the darkness I began to walk, not having a destination in mind. Perhaps, I would find an upturned cart to shelter under. Perhaps, I would find a bridge over water, a place to hide myself from the elements.

A misting rain was falling, droplets almost suspended in the air. It was spring—spring, in the Royal City, and where would I rest my head, and what would I have to eat? How would I feed myself without the mercy of the master of The Belled Dancer?

A sell-sword I was, and he was impressed by me. A sell-sword, and I had been housed at no cost. The hoodlums had the open air… what did I have?

Through the darkness a white form appeared, a scantily clad prostitute in little more than a smock, her face painted white to hide the telltale sores, her lips painted red so bright and vivid she was like a jester or a fool.

"Seigneur," said the prostitute, "shall you want a night of pleasure?"

I batted her away… stumbled forward, and nearly fell. The liquid gold was flowing through my veins, the tall glasses of ale, and I needed to relieve myself, yes, I did.

I wandered on, leaving the prostitute behind, making my way down a street in the light of the moon.

~

The squalor increased, overturned carts, garbage in piles. And the streets were stained with the remnants of chamber pots, even where they had been cleaned. The homes leaned into the street, forming a tunnel of sorts.

At last I saw the river appear before me, the River Zaros on which the city was built. The islets of the River Zaros appeared, on which were built structures, bridges… in the distance the Lady's Cathedral, the nation's symbol. And far beyond was the Royal Castle, a thing of towers and spires, stretching above even the tallest of the city's buildings, in view of the squalor and filth.

I raised my right fist. I shouted, "You owe me money, King Bretagne!

"And now I have nowhere to sleep!"

A voice called out: "I know where you can find accommodations."

I turned in view of the voice, and there standing just feet away was a woman who did not belong, a woman in a fine gown of fustian. Her clothing was dark; her hair was dark; her eyes were dark. But from her ears hung earrings studded with diamonds, and on her pale fingers were rings of gold and silver. No, she did not belong on this squalid street.

And as she stared at me, I drew a bit back.

"You are Lorkdan, aren't you?" the woman said. "The underworld's champion? The man who overthrew the count of Valle by himself? The mighty swordsman from the East?"

And I did not know what to say to her. I only knew that she didn't belong and she stuck out like an ivory statue among dross.

She was rich, amid squalor—and she knew my name.

As I stood there, I could feel myself grow dizzy, my legs grow unsteady, and I was leaning to one side and then another. I had nothing against which to steady myself.

And in my ale-clouded mind, I was trying to make sense of this enigma, a rich woman standing amid trash and squalor, one who knew my name, one who desired to know me.

"Aye," I told her. "I am Lorkdan.

"And if you know of accommodations, I would be glad to hear it."

"It comes at a cost," said the woman, in perfect diction.

How late was it? How dangerous was the neighborhood? She bore no dagger or knife, nor did a bodyguard protect her.

I wondered if I was imagining her, if the liquid gold had poisoned my mind so much that I was seeing things. But no, I wasn't imagining her—she really was there, ahead of me, on this dark spring night, amid the squalor of the Royal City.

"All things come at a cost," said the rich woman. "Nothing

is free. I am Allórie. I can offer you accommodations at my manse, but for a price."

"And food, too," Lorkdan said.

"Food," the woman Allórie said, "and drink, too… drink, which I have heard you are so fond of."

Not only had the rumors of my overthrow of the Count of Valle spread… so, too, had my love of drink.

I peered into the woman's eyes, and I had no reason to trust her, no reason to think her intentions were good. She was out here in the night, amid the darkness of the stars and moon… and she could be a phantom, a ghost, a blood-drinking spirit. But I had no place to rest my head, no shelter to hide under.

"Aye," I said to her, "I… I will…"

Allórie's eyes seemed to darken and to twinkle at the same time, and the smile she now bore revealed a set of bright white teeth. I began to get a whiff of her perfume, mountain pine and harsh liquids. And I drew near to her, and saw something else in her—a hungry fire.

Through the trash and refuse of the street we traveled, passing by beggars sitting idle on the pavestones. It was not long before we were at her manse—and a manse it was, protected by a bronze gate. It was three stories, taking up half a city block, and next to it were the glittering waters of the River Zaros.

Her servants called out—the gate ground open. She had many men of arms at her beck and call, but I knew I could dispatch them quickly, and I was sure she knew that, too.

The house's mounting levels led up to a roof that was of wooden tile. The window gables were painted green, the surface of the house white. In the yard was a bubbling fountain. And the hungry fire in Allórie's eyes had grown.

~

The walls of the home were painted in vivid floral colors. The floors of the home were teak. So far from the street, the city's stench was lessened, and further lessened by the aromatic jars of perfume that lay near the door.

"Lorkdan!" said Allórie. "I was in my bedchamber. I saw you stumbling down the road. And I knew your face.

"I knew you could help me!"

A servant was approaching from the dark of the hallway.

"Marchionette," said Allórie. "Go fetch our Lorkdan some food. What will you eat?"

It was shelter that I had wanted most… a roof under which to sleep, away from the misting rain and the dangers of the streets.

"Pudding," I said.

"Pudding," Allórie said dryly. "Go fetch our man some pudding."

She seemed humored by my choice.

"We have no pudding," said the servant.

"Well? Make some!"

~

With my stomach full and my thirst slaked, my body having had all its needs satisfied, Allórie pulled me away, up a set of marble stairs, to her bedchamber. And I saw what it was she wanted, at least in part.

In bed I climbed, and through the night I heard, in sleeping and in waking, Allórie utter the words, "Briar Rose… Briar Rose…"

Chapter Two: Briar Rose

I woke and it was late morning. Allórie was nowhere in sight. Rain was pouring, heavier than before, patting on the roof. Beyond the window, a spear of lightning crackled; moments later, thunder rolled. And for a moment, my mind adjusted; my eyes focused on where I was, and what I had done.

I was not in The Belled Dancer—I had been kicked out. I was not in The Belled Dancer—and I had been on the street. The splitting headache indicated what I had done last night, and other things were indicative as well.

On my tongue, in the dark cloudy morning, amid the storm, were the words I had heard the woman Allórie say, "Briar Rose… Briar Rose…"

What had she meant amid our lovemaking, and afterwards, when she had fallen asleep and I had lain awake?

"Briar Rose," I said to myself, aloud, and as if I had summoned up some phantasm or hungry ghost, through the door Allórie walked, still garbed in black.

Her eyes, dark yet bright, looked upon me. "Lorkdan, vagabond," she said, and lightning flashed, and thunder rolled.

"Why do you call me that, Allórie?" I said, and she smiled.

Her eyes twinkled all the more. "You are a mighty swordsman, mightier than any I know—but you were wandering in the streets, in the dark, a ruffian full and true.

"We will see if you are of use to me."

"Haven't I already been of use?" I said. And my aching body indicated it was so.

"No," said Allórie, "more I require of you… Lorkdan, vagabond."

"Briar Rose," I said softly, though I knew not why.

"Briar Rose," said Allórie. "Yes, that is what I want of you. That is what I seek.

"Come, walk with me, Lorkdan, vagabond… be my bodyguard, and much more richness awaits you. Sumptuous foods and rich ales, and other pleasures as well—if you will do my will."

"And pudding," I said.

Allórie giggled. "Yes… and pudding."

~

Amid the gusting winds and blowing rain, the distant rolls of thunder, amid the squalor of the city streets, I indeed was serving as the woman Allórie's bodyguard, and perhaps also, her paramour. The rain did not bother her, for she clutched in her hands a parasol, but I would not duck underneath of it. I would not shrink back at a little water. I was too proud.

"This city," Allórie said, "this city… by the gods, Lorkdan, can you see why people of means have a home here but stay away as much as they can? See this trash? See this garbage? See these ruffians, these vagrants?"

She was walking alongside a ruffian.

"A home here," she said, "to do business… a house in the country to live in.

"I only come to the Royal City on business."

"What business?" I said. "What business are you on?"

"Say it again, Lorkdan, vagabond. *Briar Rose…*"

"Briar Rose," I said.

Lightning flashed; thunder rolled.

~

At the Wharfs, the woman Allórie began to divulge a bit of information, what she was willing to share.

"I own several public houses in this city," she said. "I hire only the best dancers… those with the most skill.

"I give them the finest dresses. I make certain they move with grace and alacrity.

"I purchase the finest wine and the finest ale at the lowest possible price. I have made myself a fortune in the Royal City, and I know that those of noble title hate the rich merchants, the bourgeoisie—but that hatred stems from envy. I have everything I want, the finest homes, ample food, the best clothing, jewelry, long-aged wine But there is one thing I don't have, Lorkdan."

This time she did not say *Lorkdan, vagabond.*

"What is it that you do not have?" I said.

"A rose," she said, "Briar Rose… I have lost my Briar Rose."

I looked at her in puzzlement. Again, lightning flashed in the distance, and thunder echoed. I did not know what she spoke of. I did not know what she meant.

Her eyes did not twinkle; they darkened.

The rain was battering her parasol, but she was a steady arm in the raging wind. The storm had not ceased; the rain from the sky was only increasing in strength.

"When I was in my youth," she said, "I had in my possession a rose of gold. It was my favorite thing in the whole world.

"Its bloom was red, as red as fresh blood. Its stem was marred by thorns. It was delicate—but it is now in the possession of another."

"Who?" I said.

"The King of Ardogne," said Allórie.

Again lightning flashed; again thunder rolled.

To the south of the Kingdom of Zarubain, where we now stood, was a place that was little known and little understood. That land jutted into the sea, and its customs were foreign, and its language was different. Few went there, and only so for a brief time—for the natives were suspicious of the foreigner, especially those of Zarubain.

"Ardogne," I said to Allórie. "You ask a lot of me."

"Do I?" Allórie said. "If you knew how precious this rose was to me, you wouldn't think so."

Who did Allórie think she was—the woman Allórie, whom I had just met, whom I did not know? "A journey there will take many days," I said, "and I am waiting for the king's call, waiting to join his army. I cannot miss that call.

"And why can't *you* go there yourself and get it, Allórie?"

"Is it not obvious?" Allórie said, "obvious, by virtue of my words? The people in Ardogne despise all like me—they hate the people of Zarubain, rich and poor, great and small. I would not be safe in their kingdom.

"But you would be, Lorkdan. You, Lorkdan, vagabond… for you are not of this kingdom; you are of the East. They would not despise you by virtue of you being there.

"You can recover my Briar Rose, which is in the King of Ardogne's possession, and in exchange, I will give you that house you just stayed in, and servants to your name."

It was a generous offer. I feared less sleeping under than the open sky than I feared the look in her eyes when I said my piece. "Allórie, you are deluded," I said, "I promised my sword to the king. I promised to be his warrior.

"My skill is war; my tool is the sword. Your tool is the leger and the abacus. I cannot be bothered to find your Briar Rose in a foreign land."

And who would promise a house in exchange for a rose of forged gold?

Allórie's eyes darkened. "Lorkdan, vagabond," she said. "You have made your choice.

"You will be a meat puppet for the king, sent to die in a war we shall surely lose, for a pittance."

"Not a pittance," I said. "Ten *libres.*"

"That's less than I have in my pocket," Allórie said. "Lorkdan, you will rue this day… when you could have become a rich man. Instead you will sleep in the open air, like a bird or a beast. You could have done this simple task for me… but no, you have not, and it will break my heart."

She seemed genuinely grieved… but who would mourn the loss of a rose? She was surely mad.

In the dark I was left, amid the pouring rain. Darkness cloaked me. I was growing hungry, and I didn't have a coin to spare.

Chapter Three: Ill News

Alone I was, and I did not know where to go. I watched Allórie's disappearing form, and as she vanished into the darkness of the buildings, I—for the first time—wondered if I had made the wrong choice. I had nowhere to sleep; I had nothing to eat, and no way to pay for it. So why had I refused?

Perhaps, I did not trust that Allórie, though she could have surely paid my way to Ardogne, and ensured that I was well fed. She could have taken care of my needs; but there were other things to consider.

My promise to the king had been a force of law; at his call, I would assemble. At his word, I would join the armies and face the full power of the Empire.

Yet care for the law had never troubled me.

Lightning flashed; thunder rolled.

I did not trust that Allórie. No, I did not trust her at all.

~

I found myself wandering the streets, amid the rain and the wind. At last, I found myself at The Belled Dancer; where else could I go?

I knocked on the double doors; a door cracked open, and the face of the guard instantly became a scowl. "Lorkdan," he snarled. "You are not welcome here. Do not come back, or I will strike you down."

He could not strike me down—but I would not challenge him; I would not spill blood in a public house, in the king's city. I would not.

I had hoped to beg, to beg for absolution, but he slammed

the door in my face.

What would I do now? Where would I go?

~

The city of Zarubad, the Royal City, was built along a great river as it emptied into the sea. The noblemen dwelled in the islets of the river; the common lived outside them. The place where the common lived was uniformly of squalor, and in the streets, garbage was allowed to collect and fester. As I traveled aimlessly, the putrescence seemed to grow, and amid the dirt and trash, flies and fleas were buzzing, which I was swatting away.

I reached, in the afternoon, a market square, but it seemed strangely overpopulated. There seemed too many people for each merchant.

"What do you mean you're out?" snapped a common woman, poor and bedraggled, in a drab gray gown.

"The harvest went poorly," said the man she was speaking to.

A poor harvest… famine. Add that to my troubles.

The woman turned away in a huff, and as I stood there, my stomach growled.

Yet there before me, in the muck, the cloudy light of day gleamed on the sparkle of metal. A coin was there, discarded by passersby, minted of silver, with the king's head on it.

I stooped down, polished it off, and saw it was a silver groat, enough for a small meal, a drink of ale—but there would be no place to rest my head. No innkeeper would put me up for a groat.

~

I went from inn to inn, groat in hand. I heard that last night, a wave of rationing had been declared in the city, that the spring crop had failed. The price for a bit of bread was now more than a groat.

Late at night, I found a dark tavern, located not far from Seagull's Wharf. There, I spend the groat on a small bowl of pottage to fill my stomach. And I feared, and I dreaded it, that the city soon would starve.

Allórie—I thought of her, and the offer she had made me. In the dim light of candles, I pondered the thought of her, and wondered if I had made a mistake. She was insulated from the world's troubles and surely had enough food.

When I had licked clean my bowl, my stomach still growled. The tavern was ill lit, and unlike the public houses, there were no entertainments, no signs of vivaciousness or joy.

I wondered what I could do, how I could earn my keep, how I could ply my trade. But the order from the king had not come, the order for his army to mobilize.

In the dark I wandered, thirsting for a drink. At last, I found a place nestled under the roof of a house.

"You owe me money, King Bretagne," I said, stomach growling, miserable in the wetness and in the pouring rain.

"You owe me money," I mumbled, though he could not hear.

To the kingdom's troubles were now added famine, in addition to war. And I wondered how long I would wait, how long I would endure this. My sword was thirsty, and so was I.

Chapter Four: Sell-Swords

In the pouring rain, I dreamed in flashes. In the open air, thunder rumbled, but at some unearthly hour, I had fallen asleep. I woke in the morning uttering words—"Briar Rose"—and hearing the news that the king at last was calling forth his army, and making his moves for war.

~

The army the king had assembled was cobbled together of mercenaries. From one corner of the world to the other he had called them, begging their aid, sending out heralds. And, I like the others, had answered that call, for the king was rich and the pay was generous.

Amid the squalor of the Royal City I traveled, until I was—in view of the Royal Castle—at a field outside the city. There, amid the green grass and the wafting wildflowers, were thousands of dark shapes, men of all sizes in armor, wearing gauntlets and bearing swords or spears. The king's men, high-ranking members of his coterie, were dressed in finery, robes and tunics of fustian, trousers that were finely pressed, with daggers that would do little better than cut holes for sewing. They were soft men—not knowing war or danger, not knowing strife or conflict.

Before me were my fellow mercenaries, and it was we who were tasked with fighting against this barbaric Empire.

They were assembled from all corners of the world, an army comprised of sell-swords. Through their helmets I could see they were of many different nations, some swarthy, some fair—some tall, some short. And the thought came to me of the peril that the kingdom was in. Was all strength spent among the sons of

Zarubain? Did they now rely on those who sold their swords for profit, who valued gold and silver and had no love of country? The sight troubled me, but I wouldn't let it bother me. I knew why I was there; I knew why I had come. I had by my own strength overthrown the Count of Valle. The king had greatly desired my sword.

And I would fight, as long as I was paid.

One of the king's men approached a stage that had been constructed on the edge of the field, from which he could leer down at the gathered mercenaries.

He was dressed in a scarlet robe, and his fingers gleamed with many gems. "Mercenaries, sell-swords from gathered lands," he said, "I have for you good news and bad! Your pay shall remain the same; you will be well-victualed—you will have a priority for grain! But your mission I am afraid has changed, by order of the king, His Majesty, Bretagne. You will not fight in the south; it is to the east of here where you shall fight."

I balked at his words. It was the height of rudeness, the height of poor leadership. During my wait, I had gathered information on the Imperials, on their fighting styles, their methods of defense, the *testudo*, the *leo*. I had primed myself for such combat. The east he had said—did he expect me to fight against my own homeland? Not a chance!

"The king's nephew has begun a rebellion," said the man, standing upon the stage. "He errs in making a claim to the throne. Jeoffre is not in the line of succession."

I recalled the swirling rumors of the Royal City, how the heir to the throne had been a man named Jeoffre, but he had been thought dead. Last year, in Jeoffre's absence, the king we called Bretagne had assumed the Lion Throne.

It was not a good use of our resources. But the king feared this rebellion. And his gold and silver coin was no better or worse than anyone else's. My coin purse would be fat and well lined. My stomach would be full. My thirst would be slaked—it would be so.

Yet others of the mercenaries seemed to be quietly grumbling, uncomfortable with this change of plans.

Jeoffre, thought dead, had been first in line for the throne. That meant his reappearance demanded his coronation. But men do not easily give up power, nor do women in the rare instances of queens regnant.

Jeoffre—he would be a dreadful foe to fight.

But I did not care for honor or succession, only the gleam of gold and silver, the lustrous metal sparkling in the sun, a roof under which to shelter my head, and a mug of ale to press against my lips.

I would do this for Bretagne, regardless of what I wanted, regardless of whatever customs and honor required.

"Ten counts have joined him in the Eastern Heartlands," said the king's man. "That is where you will go."

My donkey Lily, holed up in a stable outside the city walls, would be put to good use. I had not seen her in many days; she would be glad of seeing her master.

I had no qualms of honor or proper succession, or paeans to the nobility of the throne. I had no use for the customs of a land of which I was not truly part. I would fight for King Bretagne, and if the would-be king Jeoffre paid me better, I would fight for him.

~

It was raining, and the roads were swamped with effluent when I reached the stables. Lily was bucking and baying at the stablemaster's touch, but when she saw me she seemed to perk up, and stopped resisting.

I rode her out of the stable, and in the meadows I could see wildflowers blooming. The air had warmed, and the sun was beginning to peek out through the swiftly-moving clouds.

My orders had been given—to County Neise I would go—I would oversee operations. The would-be king had returned, and the Count of Neise was the greatest of his friends.

As I traveled, I thought of the night I had slept under the stars, the first time in my life without a roof over my head.

As I rode on Lily down the swiftly rising muddy path, I envisioned the woman Allórie's black eyes. And I said, as misting rain again once began to pour, under my breath, *"Briar Rose."*

Chapter Five:
A Storm of Steel

The roads in the Eastern Heartlands were not easily traversed. Bridges over rivers and streams were often in rough repair, and would creak and threaten to break under the weight of Lily's hooves.

As I traveled with the mercenaries, we talked, and I realized there were many countries represented among them, some of Ardogne, some of Badelgard, some even of the Empire we had been ostensibly called to fight.

One night, in the light of the fire, somewhere just west of County Valle, as I roasted a sausage on a stick in the fire, one of the mercenaries I was sitting near drew closer.

His helm was pronged, like a lobster, forged of dark steel. At his side was a battle axe, and behind it a tower shield. He was tall, taller even than me. He would be a mighty foe on the battlefield.

"You," said the mercenary, "where are you from?"

"The east," I said, "so far east you may not know of it."

"A sell-sword?" the mercenary said.

"Aye," I said, "I am here for one reason and one reason alone… my coin purse is not heavy enough for my liking."

"To each his own," said the mercenary. "As for me, the Empire conquered my people. Turned them into slaves. I will have my revenge."

"Not, it seems, now," I said.

"Not yet," the mercenary said. "But the pay is good, and I am sure our aggression will be turned to the south soon enough."

I was not so sure.

But through the night I learned the man's name was Pago,

that he was from a region called Varengia, which I had never heard of, that he had been "a warrior for the Utes" and that he had a family afar, awaiting his return. It was more than I could say— besotted and lingering in taverns and public places, dallying long with courtesans and women of ill repute.

~

Dawn broke, and our caravan pressed on. Lily's obstinance seemed to be growing, and often, I'd have to kick her and coax her to go this way or that, or stop her from chewing on the grass, or bucking at Pago's mule. Rain turned to mix clouds, mixed clouds to sunshine. A bridge appeared at which soldiers were stationed, but those men-at-arms screamed and fled away at the sight of us, and in the span of an instant we were in the county called Neise, and in the darkness of a great wood.

Amid the shade of the elms, it was cool. One of the mercenaries began to loose his arrows at the fleeing men-at-arms, but none struck home.

I had heard rumor as I was passing along the way that more counts besides the Count of Neise were threatening to join the rebellion, that others were set to recognize Jeoffre as the true king. But here, in this county through which we had just passed, was the center of the rebellion, where its most fervent supporters could be found. They would be ripped out root and branch, and burned up in the fire—that was what the king's men had said, and that is, I suppose, what we would do. Mercenaries were not patriots; mercenaries did not have love for this king or that king. Our loyalty was to our coin purses. But we were professionals.

I had been paid as I agreed, and so I would fight. The rations had not been bread, but meats and pottage—yet my stomach was full, and I would not complain.

I began to order the mercenaries about—the mercenaries

who had seemed to acquire respect for me over the long march, and whom I had inevitably been considered the leader of. Some I told to guard the bridge; others I said to join me, and lay siege to the castle where Jeoffre was hiding away.

But amid the darkness of the elms and the faint sunshine, a dark shadow made itself known—Pago with his lobster-like helm, now bearing his battle-axe and tower shield at the ready.

"Who do you fancy yourself?" said Pago. "Our king?

"You are not our king—not our leader."

The king's men had been relatively clear who answered to who, and that I was in charge of this excursion in County Neise.

I stared Pago in the eye. "Don't test me," I said. "You'll regret it."

He rattled his battle-axe, but it was not worth my time. If we turned against each other, Jeoffre's men would kill us all, and quickly. So I backed down, acquiesced to his arrogance, his careless words—for now. If I had met him in the gutters of the Royal City, he would be lying bleeding on the ground now already, split open, my sword having plunged artfully in through the folds in his armor.

"Not a leader," I said, "not *your* leader—but I know a thing or two about battle."

Pago's eyes darkened and grew stormy. He pursed his lips—afar it seemed he glared at me, haughty, proud.

"You know a thing or two about battle," said Pago, "but have you stared into the eyes of a youngling, knowing you would have to kill her? Have you put to the sword villages and towns, slaughtering every living thing within it?"

That had not been our goal, I thought. We were to storm the castle through whatever means, surprise them—kill Jeoffre— and dispose of him in the river. Wanton violence and bloodshed was not our goal.

But as I stood there in the light of the spring day, I could see that the other mercenaries were coalescing around Pago's leadership, that they respected him more than they did me.

And the line of command would be broken. I would have to submit to it, or else I would not receive my pay.

Between my pride, and a fat coin purse, I knew what my choice would be.

I backed off our confrontation, and I allowed Pago to make his demands, telling the mercenaries from Zarubain to marshal in this or that line, the mercenaries from the Empire in another, those from Varengia in another. And we made our approach, not knowing what awaited us, through the forests and the trees, the meadows and the open fields where wildflowers bloomed.

~

As the day began to wane, the forest fell away, and in the span of an instant we were in farmland where spring wheat had grown—but that spring wheat was wilted and browned, overcome with fungus. And as suddenly as we entered those fields, a force met us, a force hundreds strong, knights galloping forth on mighty warhorses, the iron of their breastplates gleaming in the sunlight. Volleys of arrows struck us; one mercenary fell.

And they were upon us.

I drew my sword and struck at the knight; sword met sword, and I twisted, and kicked him off balance. He fell to the ground and I stabbed mercilessly, until through brute force I found a weakness in the armor, and plunged my blade straight through.

I was now spattered in blood.

I vaulted over, struck at a horse; sword met sword, but I twisted mine and disarmed him. I pilloried him with slashes and thrusts, at last removing his head from his mortal coil. He and his horse fell in a crash.

In the wind I stood there, in the sunny day, as the

mercenaries began to slowly claw back lost ground.

But I knew this was just a party to harass us, to harry us and weaken us before we reached the full force of Jeoffre's sympathizers, and that the castle's fall would be difficult, if not impossible, with the equipment we had.

A mercenary went down with a cry, pierced straight through by one of the knight's swords. Arrows fell like rain, and more mercenaries collapsed. Another volley came, and the arrow lodged itself into one of my plates of armor.

With a shout, I burst free of the ranks, and charged the archers who were operating from a high hill. I sprinted with all due speed, and they turned and fled, but I even in my armor was swifter than they—I was the better athlete, the better warrior.

My cuts and thrusts were like a storm, a rending of steel. My movements were like a dance, hopping and jolting to this side and the next. And by the end of it, the archers lay bleeding at my feet, gushing blood, and far away, in the distance, I could see the force of mercenaries had prevailed.

In the sunlight they were standing, and Pago seemed to stand the tallest among them. He was walking ahead, and he was in my sight—smiling.

"A job well done!" said Pago. "You have saved many lives, Lorkdan."

Mercenaries were finishing off the wounded, plunging their swords and spears and axes into their bodies. The horses they took for themselves or set free.

The sun was dimming, and twilight was approaching, when the mercenaries began to regather around Pago.

Pago pointed to the villages, two of which were visible in the horizon. "See all they that live there? Put them to the sword… leave none alive."

I was not averse to war, nor was I innocent of its horrors,

but when I heard Pago's words I balked.

"Anyone who does not comply will be sorry," said Pago.

And the king's man who was with us, garbed in finery, looked at Pago meekly, and said nothing to resist.

I felt appalled by his words, and appalled by his command, but after a moment's hesitation the mercenaries obeyed, scrambling down the hill toward the villages and fields where peasants were still working—not principled warriors or soldiers of the Crown anymore in my view but murderers and thugs. That was what they were—cold-blooded killers and nothing more.

I staggered ahead, down the hill, intending to make a show but not participate.

Part Two

The scenes I witnessed in the villes of Aurange and Lys were ones I cannot and will not forget. Slaughter, blood, degradation, ending in the ruin of those villes and the ruinations of the souls of Pago's men.

—Lorkdan, "Records from Evre Prison"

Chapter Six: St. Garroth's Day

In twilight, I watched the slaughter, the buildings burning, the bodies twitching, underneath a red sky that seemed as fire. And I was appalled, and as one of the mercenaries stood up from his victim, I could see shame in his eyes—deep shame. How could he absolve himself of such a crime? How could he possibly assuage his conscience? If I had taken part in the carnage, the burned buildings, the slaughtered and degraded innocents, a hundred meetings with a priestess could not take away the guilt, nor prayers said to the gods.

It appalled me. The houses were burning and bodies lay everywhere. The peasants of those towns had done nothing wrong.

Of all people, all the mercenaries I saw, only Pago seemed free of shame. He was haughty, gleeful, even proud of what he had done, what he had caused his underlings to do.

What a legacy… what shame. What horror had been done this night.

I felt I had seen my limit. I wanted to turn back—I was tempted even to do so.

But the king's man responsible for paying us did not seemed bothered. His expression was stone cold, free of emotion, consenting to all of Pago's decisions… his decisions, which had led to all this horror.

Towers of smoke were rising from the burning of the villages. I thought of returning to the east.

But instead my mind turned again to the gold and to the silver. I wondered if it was worth that price; and I decided it was.

The clouds were cloaked in purple; the sun was dipping below the farm fields and elms. I knew I would not leave; I would not let up in my desire for gold. But what horror had been committed here, what a crime against gods and man. Under their breath, I said a prayer—even to the one I favored, Balzor, god of the underworld and of death. For even he would not wish to see carnage like this. Even he would not want such cruelty and wanton violence, such indignity in death.

~

The next day, we resumed our march, and the disgust did not leave me, and the horror was lingering, the utter revulsion.

The sun was bright, the sky clear and cloudless. Birds were chirping, jays and robins—did they know what had happened? How could they chirp and sing their song in the wake of what had occurred in those twin villages? How could they chirp and sing their song after so many had died, in such indignity, and for no reason at all?

One thing I was sure… something was wrong with Pago. And I had begun to question everything about him.

Was he really of a place called "Varengia?" Did the Empire really enslave his people?

The pay we were given assuaged my concerns, two more silver coins falling into my coin purse, plus what food could be found.

We made our approach to the castle, and I did my best to forget everything I had seen.

~

More skirmishes followed as we traveled through the fields, forests, and hills, past villages that Pago—thank the gods—ignored out of haste. We set fires to the farm fields, the wheat and the grain and any green growing thing standing in our way.

More skirmishes followed, but these battles ended quickly,

for we moved too swiftly for Jeoffre's men to intuit our movements.

I recalled my mission—to put an end to Jeoffre, toss his body in the River Garre, and then be done.

But I also realized that as soon as we finished with this mission, and the war with the nation called the Empire began, I would have to fight alongside these people. I would have fight with these people whom I had seen commit acts of incredible violence and violation, who had obeyed Pago without flinching, who had done his dark deeds, and defiled themselves in the process.

The road was winding up and down a hilly country when, in the distance, a castle appeared, a plain thing of stone surrounded by villages and more farm fields. It was the seat of the Count of Neise and where, according to the king's men, Jeoffre was being hidden.

The castle's towers stretched toward the sky; and the peasants were going about their business, tending to their sheep and cows and pigs, seemingly not aware of us, or perhaps forced to work in spite of the danger.

"Charge!" cried Pago, and I agreed with his command, but I feared for those poor peasants in the fields and what would befall them. I had seen what this company of mercenaries was capable of.

~

In the span of an hour, the castle was surrounded by mercenaries on all sides. Amid wanton bloodshed and burnings, the peasant villages were burned to ash. But in the wan sunlight, our attentions were diverted—though the peasants received the full force of our arms, they were not our focus; and so Pago's cruelty was restrained.

We spent the remainder of the day assembling fortifications

around the sight of the siege, for fear a company of knights would sally forth to break us and scatter us.

Now was the hard task of siege-craft—waiting.

Eventually, hunger or thirst would drive them out. Eventually, they would surrender without a fight.

But as twilight set, there was a gleam in Pago's eye, and he began to order the other mercenaries to gather wood to build ladders and battering rams. Did he really intend to storm the castle, and risk the mercenaries' lives? I supposed I was not surprised.

That gleam in his eyes seemed to brighten; up ahead, there was noise.

~

A woman had appeared on the battlements, a woman with long gold hair and brilliant eyes. The gown she wore was rose-colored, and of silk. She was clearly a noblewoman, a woman of importance and means. Her green eyes were filmed with tears.

"My brother—the heir… of the House of Bretagne… he returns from a pilgrimage to a stolen throne! And not only will my uncle not abdicate—he intends to kill his own blood."

The mercenaries began to heap abuses at her. Pago was the loudest. "Surrender now, woman! Or you will come to wish you were dead!"

I knew what that meant, and it seemed the woman did, whose lips puckered in disgust. "May the Goddess strike you dead!" she said. "May she forever curse my uncle's throne!"

"The gods cannot save you!" shouted Pago. "No one can save you now, woman, except yourself! Let us in, and we will let you live!"

She spat at us from afar, and her spittle struck one of the mercenaries on his helmet.

"The Goddess curse you!" shouted the woman. "The Goddess smite you! The Goddess strike my uncle from his throne!"

And she vanished from view, disappearing into the castle's stone corridors.

A dark smile had grown over Pago's face, perhaps in anticipation of what lay ahead.

~

In the morning a party of knights indeed arrived, hundreds strong, from an outlying county. Upon our wooden fortifications, hastily built, they did their best for battle, striking one mercenary dead, then another, impaling one on a lance—cutting another down with the sword.

But the sally broke upon our combined forces, with the help of our fortifications, and they fled off on horse into the woods and the smoldering remnants of fields. The hunger in the castle that was called Castle Dairre was surely growing. But I know Pago had crueler, and more dangerous plans.

At night, Pago oversaw the construction of more battering rams, and also a ladder. The time for action was at hand—but if we were merely patient, the resolution could be peaceful. No one in the castle would have to die… no one, I suppose, save the would-be king Jeoffre.

At dark, at some unearthly hour, the construction was stopped. But as we were preparing to retire, to sleep in shifts, a light appeared above—not the moon's light, but a fainter one, a candle.

The woman was back, the golden-haired, green-eyed sister of Jeoffre. She clutched in her arms a babe, and at her side was her husband.

It was a ploy for sympathy—but Pago was a monster, and he had a monstrous heart.

"Mercenaries!" she said. "Sell-swords! Jeoffre has agreed to a deal—he will drop his claims to the throne, if you will only let him live!"

"We accept"—that is what I wanted to say, but I kept silent.

The king's man was asleep, the one authorized to speak on his behalf.

But from the night darkness a shadow arose, tall—still wearing his lobster-like helm, Pago.

"A curse on you, woman!" Pago said. "Your Jeoffre has already shown himself a traitor! And traitors deserve death!"

The woman wailed, and again retreated into the darkness with the babe she clutched, followed by her paramour.

A wind was blowing; and clouds were veiling and then unveiling the moon. The air was growing cold; I recalled it was St. Garroth's day, the only feast day for the god of the underworld. Under my breath I prayed, and then I retreated to my tent, and I slept. I had dreams of a bloodlit sky, a red sun, and clouds colored like flesh.

Chapter Seven:
The Siege

We stormed the castle the next day, and the mercenaries took turns pummeling the gate with the battering ram. The defenders on the castle were few and their strength was faint; but bravely they fought, including the woman's paramour, her husband; and other family members, now suited in armor and bearing swords and axes and maces and flails. Servants poured vats of boiling water to delay us, but doom was writ for the castle called Castle Dairre; doom was inevitable, yes, doom. And they knew it—their faces showed it.

Mercenaries began to set their ladders upon the walls, even as the men with the battering rams heaved their weapons against the doorway. As for me, I offered little better than moral support, though I had begun to despise all this, and despise the sight of this reckless incursion. Was my heart growing soft? No—I thought of gold and silver, gleaming coins, and took my sword in hand, and began to shimmy up a ladder. I bowled past mercenaries as I did, moving with all due speed. One of the castle servants dumped boiling water but that boiling water fizzled and steamed and dripped off my plates of armor. Swords met me—and the strike of a flail. But I vaulted over the battlements and at once took to my task— the task I had been hired for. I was nothing if not a professional.

I struck and I parried—I impaled a man at arms with my sword, breaking deftly through a hole in his armor. I battered the man with the flail, and pilloried him with many strokes, until at last I drew blood. A storm of steel—as before—and I did not remember where or whence I struck, but at the end of it many were bleeding and dying, and the rest had fled.

The paramour of Jeoffre's sister, her husband, was looking at me in horror, eyes slowly blinking. "Run," I said, in a low voice, so as not to be heard by the mercenaries scaling the ladder.

Run, I had said—and he did, bolting through the open door.

Mercenaries were now climbing the wall, entering the castle proper, and nothing now could be done by the defenders. The battle was now won, thanks to Lorkdan. I was the consummate professional.

Now was the hardest part, to put aside my moral qualms, to do what was asked of me. I entered the castle, and when I questioned what I was doing, I remembered coins of gold and silver, and bubbling ale, and food to fill my stomach.

~

In the castle we were met with more resistance, warriors pouring out from every dark corner, common servants becoming warriors and beating at us with bats and striking at us with knives and daggers. Those servants fared poorly; the warriors not much better. The castle called Castle Dairre was now being swarmed with the worst company, but what fear they had now was not enough. I had seen what Pago and the others were capable of, in the villes of Aurange and Lys. The peasants in those villes had done nothing wrong—but Jeoffre and his family and their servants had dared resist, and injured a few. What horrors awaited them now?

I traveled on, striking with my sword, jabbing with my feet, attempting to scare the pitiful servants and the outmatched warriors and not draw blood. I hoped they would be shown mercy but I knew none would come.

At last, we pushed past them, found ourselves in the great hall, now filled with mercenaries—bread and wine free for the taking, upturned tables and chairs—and through a locked door, the throne rocm.

It took a little while for the mercenaries to transport the battering ram. But when they did, I watched from afar, wincing—knowing that Jeoffre and his family were behind that door.

And in the distance, near that door, I could see the husband of Jeoffre's sister, her paramour, bleeding on the ground, pierced many times by a sword, white and drained of blood. If he was not dead, he was on death's door.

Crack came the door, bursting apart, shuddering and collapsing into its component parts. Screams echoed from within the room, but the mercenaries poured in, smiling—their eyes bright, their complexions bright with glee.

I entered after a short delay.

Chapter Eight: The Choice

In the throne room was Jeoffre's sister, her babe clutched at her side.

With her were men and women, boys and girls, of varying ages.

And on the throne was who I presumed to be Jeoffre.

I was stunned by the sight of him—staggered, perhaps—for he was not what I presumed him to be.

He was a boy, not a man, and he could not have seen ten years in his young life. He was dressed in a neat black robe, and on his brown hair was a gold crown. In his hand was a miniature scepter.

He was innocent. He had returned from a pilgrimage, his sister said.

This rebellion, this gambit for the throne… his claim was legitimate, but I was certain it had not been his idea. It had been impressed on him; he was just a boy. It had been impressed upon him—and by whom?

His sister was sobbing, clutching her babe. Jeoffre did not seem aware of the situation he was in.

And the room was going quiet. A dark shadow emerged, and the mercenaries parted before him—a lobster-like helm, a battle-axe. Pago.

His eyes were gleaming; he was smiling. He had the look of a hungry wolf, or a cat playing with its meal. I supposed he would enjoy this. But I wouldn't.

He strode up before the makeshift throne. He leaned on his battle axe.

"A traitor, Jeoffre, that is what you are; a traitor to the Crown and the kingdom—and traitors deserve death."

But Pago turned—and no longer did Jeoffre have his attention. His eyes sparkled, and the gleam in his eyes seemed to grow.

"Jeoffre must be killed. His blood must be spilled this day. It must be so. And we have here someone who considers himself more righteous than us. He considers himself more moral, more pious... and I think he should do the honors...

"Lorkdan... step forward!"

And I did step forward, sword in hand, and I began to tremble.

"Lorkdan!" said Pago. "Kill this Jeoffre."

And I realized, in that moment, that if I disobeyed, I'd at best be forced out of the king's service, and worse may yet befall me. I walked ahead, and tried to conjure up images of gold and silver coins fattening my coinpurse.

I walked ahead. I raised my sword. Jeoffre at that moment realized what was happening, and began to cower on his makeshift throne. I drew near—saw the terror in his eyes.

"Do it!" urged Pago.

But my hand was trembling; my breath was shallow. I'd grown lathed in cold sweat.

I drew near; and tried to think of gold, and of silver. And I tried to remember what would happen to me if I failed, if I did not carry out the mission that was the reason I had traveled here.

I had killed people who did not deserve it before. My sword was rarely thirsty. Yet peering into Jeoffre's eyes, I found myself strangely immobile.

At last I turned around. I peered into Pago's eyes.

"He is a child, Pago," I said.

Pago's smile grew. "A coward you are... and now a traitor to the king's name. Don't think you'll escape punishment, Lorkdan."

I walked, and then I hurried. I hurried, and I ran. I departed the castle to the sound of an anguished cry. And outside, I could see the sky had darkened, that clouds had rolled in, that lightning was flashing and peals of thunder were rising over the landscape.

~

In the pouring rain, on Lily, my donkey, I headed off down the road, burdened by my decision, wondering if I had made the right choice.

Yes, I had. I had made the correct the decision, the only one I could live with. Old Lorkdan had grown soft.

I turned Lily east, headed home, back to the world I had forgotten, the town of Berry Thicket, where I had been born. It would be a long journey, but it was the only place I'd be safe.

~

Amid the thunder, I felt assailed, not by the lightning or the rain, nor by the wind which was blowing west, against me. I felt assailed by memory, by the thought of the woman Allórie and the darkness of her eyes, by the strange request which lingered in mystery.

"Briar Rose," I said and the winds seemed to gust in response.

"Briar Rose." Lightning flashed; thunder rolled.

The green hills stretched before me. The bridge that would take me east lay just ahead. Lily seemed eager for the first time ever, eager to plod on, and at last it was I who jerked on her reins to stop her.

"Briar Rose," I said, and though I did not know why, I made an inexplicable decision, one that came from the heart and not the mind, one based on a fleeting feeling, and the memory of a pretty woman's eyes.

"Briar Rose," I said, and the winds gusted, and lightning flashed, and thunder rolled.

"Briar Rose," I said, and turned Lily around despite her protest, and kicked her with my shins. Westward we went, back to the Royal City, back to danger—not for reasoned thought, but because of the memory of a woman, and two words, *briar rose.*

Chapter Nine: Returning

When I reached the Royal City, days later, I put up Lily in the same stable. But the stable-keeper seemed different now, paler, gaunter—unhealthy. And he said little when I offered him my coin, and almost seemed to glare.

"Lorkdan," he said.

And I wondered if, under his breath, he had uttered *Lorkdan, vagabond.*

~

The Royal City was no longer bustling; the people moved about slowly, and the energy seemed to have dissipated. The faces of the common in the Outer City appeared gaunt, and the music in the public houses, which had continued day and night, seemed fainter now. Before, I could hear the sounds of such revelry far outside the door.

But revelry seemed far from the city I had walked into. Revelry and entertainment and excitement were the furthest thing from the people's minds it seemed, poor, bedraggled, shifting about and not walking. And I remembered—the famine.

The rains had continued, and the winds were whipping, when I found myself at the door of The Belled Dancer. I could hear no music, and I could see that the door was locked. The filth of the city streets seemed to have piled up even more, and the squalor seemed to have been taken to a new height. I crossed the alleyways and the narrow streets, passing by the houses that leaned over each other and formed almost a tunnel. I walked by wild dogs and children, and common city dwellers walking to and fro, until at last I was at the house of the woman Allórie.

Lightning flashed; thunder rolled.

And the winds were gusting into a storm.

I made my approach; I walked to the door. Thrice I knocked, I waited.

Lighting flashed and thunder rolled.

The door opened, and standing there was the woman Allórie, with eyes by turns dark and bright.

"Lorkdan, vagabond," she said, and the lightning briefly painted her face in blue light.

"Not so," I said.

"Why have you come?" said Allórie.

And I said to her, "Briar Rose."

Part Three

What she told me made no sense. But I was compelled to do it, as if by a spirit or a ghost. And it struck me at times that she could be a sorceress; but would a sorceress so vainly chase after a rose of gold?

—Lorkdar, "Records from Evre Prison"

Chapter Ten: The Narrow Stream

"The Briar Rose is in the possession of the King of Ardogne," said the woman Allórie.

"It is made of gold—but its bloom is red, red like a real rose. Red like blood."

Her request was no less baffling. It made little sense that a woman wanted a false rose of gold so badly. She was willing to spend a fortune to get it—her house in the city, and to that price she had added ten *libres*—that was one-hundred *deniers*.

"I will get it for you," I said, "that I promise… you have my word."

Allórie smiled. "You will know it when you see it. You will recognize the Briar Rose."

Briar Rose… a rose of gold, with a red bloom—in the possession of the King of Ardogne. It was a fanciful tale, but Allórie in addition to my reward would pay my way there. I would be well suited to complete this rich woman's task.

~

The air was cold when I departed, and the rain had the character of sleet. On Lily, I rode steadily southwards, and the stink and squalor of the Royal City fell away to suburban villes and scattered woods, followed by farm fields whose peasants were laboring in the soil. The withered wheat was no good, the apple trees looked sickly, and famine was in the land. And it struck me as I rode on Lily, bucking and braying and resisting, southwards through the region called Vale Royeau, that the nobles and the rich merchants looked down on the peasants—but it was they that sustained the kingdom. If they failed or if a disease of plant spread, everything was brought to a standstill, from the Royal City to every town and ville. And I uttered a prayer though my god was the god of the underworld, for their protection, that they would turn it all around, that the plants would overcome the disease, or that the next harvest would be better. A nation that was readying to go to war was in no shape for hunger or famine. If the strength of the sons of Zarubain were spent, they could not fight anyone.

Days passed, days and nights. Sometimes, I would sleep in my tent, but other times I would not bother, sleeping outside in my bedroll or just a blanket. Allórie had told me in the vaguest terms where I should go, but it was my responsibility to find my way to the kingdom called Ardogne.

One evening, in a region called the Duchy Lessant, at the side of the road a public house appeared, and by it a stable. I thought of ale sparkling in the glass, and sausages baked in pudding. And though it was not in my interest to delay—my money was finite; my resources were not unlimited—I found I could not resist.

For days, my tongue had grown dry, and I had filled my stomach on road-bread and salt pork. I wanted something more, and so close to Ardogne's border, perhaps I could hear of something, some news, some morsel of information that would aid the mission I had undertaken for the madwoman Allórie, who wanted her "Briar Rose."

The public house was also an inn, and its sign was painted in the form of a motley fool. Fragrant lavender was growing in its yard, and ivy covered its plaster walls. It was nestled between two trees that were also blossoming. The servants had a gaunt look, but they came to me readily, and without a word, hauled the resistant Lily into the stable.

And I entered the inn and public house with the sign of the

motley fool.

~

The room was dark and it was empty, save for those that worked there. The serving girl had almost a glare on her face when I entered.

"Who goes there?" she said.

"Lorkdan," I answered.

"Lorkdan," she said, "the underworld's champion?"

Was my name known here, even in this inn, this inn that time forgot? This obscure inn, on the side of the road, was aware of my exploits in County Valle and elsewhere.

"I heard that the king wants a word with you," she continued.

It seemed she was privy to that knowledge—and if a serving girl in some obscure inn in the "Duchy Lessant" knew I was in trouble with the king, then everyone did.

Word spread so fast. It spread faster than Lily's slow and obstinate gait.

I was in trouble with the king. He "wanted a word with me"—perhaps, because I had refused to kill an innocent boy, Jeoffre, his nephew. Some called me a vagabond—but was anyone of worse character than he who sat on the Lion Throne?

"Will you serve me nonetheless?" I said to her.

"All are served in The Laughing Jester—all who pay." Her tone had a hard edge.

I took my seat.

"What will you have?" said the serving girl.

"Sausage," I said.

"We have none," she replied.

"Bread," I said.

"One *sou*," she said.

"You're kidding," I said—it was more than most made in a few days' wages.

"Two *sous* with butter," she went on.

I gawked. But I ordered it nonetheless. And my coin-purse, fattened by the woman Allórie, got a little lighter.

"Ale, too," I said, and I dreaded hearing its price. But she ferried a glass from the cellar and brought me hot bread.

And when my thirst was slaked, and I had ordered another ale, I said to the serving girl, "Have you heard news of Ardogne?"

~

"Ardogne," she said, and she was like a storm embodied. Hot anger gleamed in her eyes. "So arrogant, so prideful… they live in a place of great beauty and they think they are superior for it. Not for culture! Not for noble lineage!

"They bask in the sun and look down on us from afar, because they were blessed with a beautiful land. But they are impoverished and they are dissolute! They are barbaric!"

And I wondered if a man from Ardogne had scorned her, or what else had caused such an upswell of emotion.

I found myself almost laughing at her outburst, the anger in her eyes, the furiousness of her words.

"King Bretagne should invade them straightaway, when we have this Empire defeated… bring them into the fold. Conquer that peninsula… bring King Diego back in chains."

King Diego—that was the name of the King of Ardogne, or so it seemed.

I realized how little I knew of the place I was traveling to.

And I ordered another ale.

"What do you know of King Diego?" I said to her, and the

liquid gold was beginning to be felt, and my once-fat coinpurse was beginning to feel light.

"A slob," she said to me. "A representative of his people… conniving, greedy, a whoremonger. And with a palace filled with courtesans."

I ordered another ale, and when she came back I said to her, "Why do you hate Ardogne so much?"

And for the first time in the night, a bit of self-reflection appeared in her eyes. "A man of Asina Aurea scorned me."

Asina Aurea… the capital, presumably. That was where I would go. That was where I would travel to.

~

From Duchy Lessant to Duchy Ajernon I traveled, past its rose-colored castle, under fair weather and sunny skies.

From Ajernon to Durance and beyond I went, and signs of the famine were growing, food impossibly expensive in the roadside inns and the scattered public houses. I began to avail myself more and more of the road-bread and the salt pork, and wondered how much silver such rations would set me back now.

The faces I saw on the road seemed gaunt and pale, and the devastation of the spring wheat was becoming clear—fields and fields, in every duchy and small county, withered and brown, not good for harvesting. And again I prayed, even to Balzor god of the underworld, that the kingdom would find its way out of the predicament, that they would emerge from this famine strong somehow, and ready to face the monstrous Empire.

As I traveled south, heat was building, and the lands began to grow drier. In places, the grass was brown, and the forests were more scattered and further apart. At a crossroads was a man-at-arms, brown of hair, with bright blue eyes. And I inquired of him for directions along the road.

"Why do you pass through Silvan March?" the man-at-arms said.

And I realized I was in Zarubain's south-westernmost region.

"Why would you go to Ardogne?" he continued.

"My business is my own," I said.

"Are you a free man?" said the man-at-arms. "Free to move about? Not a serf? Not bound to some lord?"

"You'll just have to take my word for it," I said.

The man-at-arms seemed suspicious, but he wouldn't dare arrest me. I was wearing some of my armor, and to my back was strapped my greatsword. Everything about me marked me as a warrior.

"West down this road… west," he said. "Take it far enough, and you'll be in Ardogne. Past the Narrow Stream.

"Give Diego my curses…"

I smiled at his words, and I thanked him. Taking Lily's reins in my hands, I urged her on, and days later, morning broke… before me was a muddy brown stream so shallow Lily could walk across it easy. Beyond that was dryness and desert.

Chapter Eleven: The Barrens

So suddenly, and in the span of an hour, I had crossed from a place of elms and ash trees and pines to a place I'd think would belong far south of the world. It was dryness; it was barrenness. And the heat was not thick and cloying, but dry and waterless.

Dusty fields stretched into the distance, and the shadows of low mountains. Water would be a precious resource and I wondered if I were risking Lily's life.

Lily, however, was making the decision for me, eagerly plodding ahead, down the road, as the road took on properties of dust and sand, and then disappeared altogether.

But how large was Ardogne? Couldn't I easily find a city the size of Asina Aurea? Surely, I could.

~

As the midday sun glared, and Lily showed signs of slowing and weakening, I beheld where I was, and couldn't make sense of this bizarre miracle of geography. West of the Narrow Stream was desert; a few miles east were forests and well-watered valleys suited for agriculture. I tried to make sense of it, but I was not much of a thinking man, no philosopher or man of learning—not by any means. I only trusted that the gods had some reason for making such a strange phenomenon of nature—but as I thought on that reason, I could see that Lily was huffing and puffing, moving slower and slower by the moment, and that she was thirsty.

~

I looked about, seeing no sign of the road—it had

disappeared with the sand. The low mountains stretched ahead, networks of them overlooking the dry dusty fields. Patches of grass could be seen, and shrubby green growths covered in thorns.

"Asina Aurea," I said – the capital. Surely, it was near.

The heat was building, the sun was glaring in my eyes, and whenever a wind would blow down from the mountains, spirals of dust would gather, and I'd cough. Lily plodded on, but as she did, I began to worry. These dry, sandy fields were so vast, and I was so isolated, so alone. I was in the middle of the wilderness, unprotected. And I was beginning to grow thirsty, and my waterskin felt light.

Coin could not save me now. Not all the money in the world could prevent the danger I was in. I could not say to the mountains—here, a loaf of bread, a glass of ale. I could not say to the green growths, "Here—a silver, for a little water." But I was beginning to grow so delirious I thought I might soon try.

As the sun's light began to wane and the heat lingered, I finished off what was left in my waterskin. I poured the remainder in my mouth… and I had never felt so isolated, so alone, amid the dusty fields and the dry, rocky low mountains.

Mountains, I thought, should have snowcapped peaks—gushing creeks and rivers, with slopes crowned in pine. But these low mountains were something different, of dry rock, high enough to be seen and to torment you—to remind you that there was no water in them.

The thirst was building and I didn't think I'd sleep—but that was the least of my concerns.

~

As I built my tent, a swarm of insects fluttered ahead—no, bats, thousands, maybe millions. And I recalled the legends of blood-sucking bats, and I wondered if those bats would drink me dry.

But they passed on into the golden twilight.

The sun set on my first day in the inexplicable desert. Darkness fell; and it was night.

~

In my tent, I tossed, I turned—I couldn't sleep. In my mind's eye, I saw the woman Allórie's dark yet bright eyes, and felt I had disappointed her. I did not know whether I had slept or only lain in my cot, but at one point it was dawn, and my eyes were open, and I was tired… tired, and thirsty, so thirsty I could think of nothing except water.

And abandoning all thought of Briar Rose, I vowed to find water if I could.

~

On Lily, who was growing tired, I at first rode her, and then gently led her, across the scorched fields. I was so thirsty I felt I was being driven mad, and in the glare of the sun I thought I saw sight of a town, but the faster I traveled after it, the faster it pulled away from me, and I realized it was a mirage, a delusion borne of lack of water.

As I traveled I was exerting myself, sweating profusely, and all that precious water was leaving my body. The hateful mountains seemed to mock me, saying, "I have no water—I am dry."

Lily's movements were growing slower and slower, until at last I was yanking her, weeping, realizing I had led that poor beast I loved here, to die. In the sun's heat, I too began to stagger, and thought to myself, Lorkdan was not a vagabond, but he was a fool for certain.

Eventually, I was dragging her, weeping and losing more water, as my boots dragged against the dirt and earth. And I realized how stupid I was, going on this quest—venturing vainly after a reward that was promised by the woman Allórie—the madwoman Allórie.

"Lily, I'm sorry," I said to her, to my donkey, and hoped she could understand my speech. "Lily, I'm sorry for leading you here… to this place. I'm not a good master after all."

When I spoke, my mouth and tongue were dry, devoid of moisture.

Why, oh why, had the gods created this inexplicable desert, when across the Narrow Stream there had been water and food and greenness and life? What trick of nature caused this? What ill wind had caused a waterless place where trees and green things should grow?

The heat was building; it was midday, and I was no closer to water. My walk had morphed to a stagger, and Lily was barely moving.

Under the sun I began to sink to my knees, and my judgment was clouded, and I was desperate yet strangely tired.

As soon as my head hit the dry dusty earth, I blacked out, reaching for Lily.

~

I woke to a storm.

Lightning flashed—no, the gleam of metal in the moonlight. Thunder rolled—no, men were shouting at me in a strange tongue.

They were ordering me up, then shoving a waterskin to my throat, which I gladly drank from, and the water pouring down my throat was like a miracle elixir, filling me with strength.

I realized they had taken my sword—but who were they?

My eyes adjusted to the dim moonlight, and I could see that before me were dusky men in loose white clothing, bearing at their sides scimitars of steel. There were about a dozen of them, all men, and near them was a hairy beast on all fours, like a horse or a donkey, but much taller than either. It was loaded with saddlebags, and I felt sorry for the creature in truth, heavily burdened in a dry and waterless place.

"I mean you no harm!" I said, first in the tongue of the East, remembering the Ardognians' hatred of the Zarubes.

"I mean you no harm!" I then said in the tongue of the Zarubes, the tongue of the kingdom I was sworn to serve.

But if the men understood my speech, they showed no sign of it.

They had disarmed me—and even I, Lorkdan, could not overcome them with my fists. It was not so.

With my thirst sated, I stood there, though my head ached and my toes and fingers felt numb. I did what they wished, and in their flowing tongue I gathered they were ordering me to follow them.

And follow them I did.

~

In the moonlight, under a cold wind, I, Lorkdan, followed the men whom I did not know without complaint. They had given me water; but sometime during the night, as I trekked through the dust and the sand, I realized my coinpurse had been removed from me.

I had been robbed—but I had been revived. Without them, I would have died, so I supposed in a way I should be thankful. But

I did not know what was happening to me; I did not know their intentions.

On I trekked, in the moonlight, underneath the stars and moon.

~

It had to be near morning when our journey stopped. Under the shade of palmettos and fan palms was a steep cliff that overlooked the raging sea. Near that cliff was a camp of finely crafted tents, together with animals and small farming plots.

Where was I?

I supposed I was in Ardogne.

But what was this? And who were these people?

They had robbed me, and they had taken my sword. But because of them, I and the beast plodding next to me—Lily—had survived. How could I not be thankful, if only a small bit?

The dawn was beginning to rise in the distance, above the sea. Women were stirring from their tents, and over their bodies they had rich crimson gowns; they were dusky, like the men, and their ears were pierced with earrings of gold. Over the necks were necklaces of gemstone and silver. Some had young babes clutched to their chests; in the open air, children began to run about, and at the sight of the palmettos, the fan palms, the sun-bathed sea, the inexplicable warmth—I pinched myself, and wondered if I was in a dream.

Chapter Twelve: Luminous

"What are you doing?" I said to them.

"Unhand me!" I said to the man standing in front of me—the chief perhaps, a man of considerable age, with more white hairs than black on his head, and dressed in a fine green robe.

His underlings were tying my hands behind my back. They were moving me toward the sheer cliffs of the sea.

"Why?" I said.

"Why?" I repeated myself in the tongue of the Zarubes.

I could see a young man playing with my coinpurse, counting the *sous* and *deniers*.

The leader, in a halting, uncertain tone, responded to me in the language that I myself had spoken. "You were found dead in the desert," he said. "You were revived... and we will properly dispose of you. You are our enemy, a Zarube... off the scarp you will go, to the sea, with the blessing of Toro."

Toro—their god, it seemed.

"Please," I said. "I am not your enemy... I am Lorkdan..."

And the warriors halted their jerking me ahead; they began to speak to themselves in their rhythmic tongue. Their leader looked at me in a new way.

"Lorkdan," he said, "of Berry Thicket."

"That's me."

~

My binds were not loosened—indeed, I was cut with a switch, and made to suffer a while. They did not feed me well, but instead a starchy porridge made from those thorny green growth's I'd seen in the Barrens.

They set me on a stool, and the leader stared me in the eye. His sword gleamed, hanging from its belt. It would appear he did not trust me. And I was soon aware that he alone, of all these people, spoke the language of the Zarubes.

"Lorkdan of Berry Thicket," he said in his rhythmic way, an accent that I had a hard time understanding. "You overthrew the Count of Vallée…"

"Valle," I corrected him, and my correction didn't seem to bother him.

Instead, he grew more serious, more sober. "We have a problem here, in Ardogne, that maybe you could solve," he said. "A false king."

Where had I heard this before?

"Diego," I said.

"No," said the leader of this tribe, and the switch struck me again—sharp and harsh, drawing blood. "Diego is the true king, but he was forced from the throne. In his place reigns his brother Jafet—and what a wicked man is Jafet.

"You overthrew the Count of Valle… you can overthrow him."

And if they viewed me as superhuman, surely they realized that if they handed me back my sword, I could quickly dispatch of them all.

But I had other reasons for entertaining their request… hadn't the woman Allórie said the Briar Rose was in possession of Diego?

"For that," I said, "I will need my sword."

"Not so fast," said the man. "I am no fool. If I am to give you back your sword, you must become one of us, one of the Via… you must know Toro, and you must honor him."

~

My hair was cut, my beard was shaved. And the leader of this Barrens tribe, the Via, whose named I learned was Andeo, began to instruct me of my duties—at dawn I was to tend to the crops in their fields, and then from noon to evening, tend to their animals, which were an assortment of cattle and sheep.

And Toro—at all times of the day I was to pray to Toro.

"Who is Toro?" I said to Andeo.

And a switch took me, and I bled.

"Toro is our god," said Andeo, "and he sends the rain… and it is his blessing that makes Diego's claim legitimate, and Jafet's false.

"He lives on the mountain near the City… Mount Ebora. He is the god of Ardogne."

The city—Asina Aurea, presumably. It was Ardogne's capital.

Knowing I could do nothing else, I set about my work. It was dawn, I was tired, but I was still at the Via tribe's mercy.

~

The crops in the plot were green shoots, and I could not make sense of what they were, but with a pail I began to water them, one after another. I bristled at the task in the Barrens heat, for it was not my purpose in life—it was not my profession. Everything about it was a strain. But as I did, I tried to discover who had taken my coinpurse, and as I watered the plants, I looked at the men and women—the young and the old—with me, and listened for the sound of jingling metal.

It was not lost on me that these people had robbed me. They were responsible for my current predicament.

They were also responsible for my survival—but they were bandits and little more. I grunted and I bristled, but in my work throughout the day I began to pick up, here and there, on words.

Vasa—water. *Elo*—the sun. *Emer*—man.

And when the sun set, and the cattle had been fed, and the night fell, torches were lit, and music began, and wine was poured, and food was served.

The lamb was so spicy my eyes watered, pungent, powerful. Even the barley oats had been doused in spices.

The women sang, and patted cymbals, to cries of "É Toro!"

The wine I did not prefer, but it had been mixed with floral honey—sweet to the tongue, and refreshing. After the backbreaking work, I was glad to slake my thirst on anything, even this. Ale was my drink, but this would do.

"Signor Lorkdan will help us!" cried Andeo, their leader, his blood clearly flowing with wine and spiced drink. "He will bring our people back from ruin!"

Normally, I would be given to drunkenness. If I had one glass, I'd have another. But knowing I was in danger, I decided to hold out as long as I could, for I did not trust these people at all, and at any moment I expected a dagger at the neck.

But the music raged on; the women in their crimson gowns, fair faced and beautiful, twirled and danced or sat down in the laps of their husbands. I was beginning to lose my sense of danger; I was beginning to lose my fear.

Through scattered comments, I began to realize that many tribes inhabited the Barrens, and that in the springtime they would sow crops, and in the summer they would wander, seeking after grass for their cattle. In the winter they would return to their crops, praying for the blessing of Toro, that they would have something besides meat and cheese to eat.

And I learned the names of others. Caros—a warrior. Sienda, his wife. And the chief priest of the tribe of Via, the devotee of Toro, was named Banos.

They seemed to be treating me as one of them. But I wasn't. And I continued scanning the camp for any sign of my coinpurse, as the feast and the revel raged on.

At last, despite my better judgment, though I'd held out longer than normal, I had another glass of sweet wine, and as I sipped, I asked Andeo, the chief of the Via, a question that had been brewing over my long day of work. "Why," I said to him, "are you so invested in Diego being king? Why do you wish me to overthrow him?"

Andeo began to speak softly. He seemed to have drunk the least of all the tribesmen, which I supposed was wise for a leader. "Diego protected the tribes, especially the Via," he said. "Jafet... he wishes to drive us to extinction."

"And where is Diego now?" I said.

"I do not know," Andeo said, "I'd hoped Lorkdan of Berry Thicket would find him."

~

In the morning, with the crops well rooted and watered, and given the best chance to thrive, I and the rest of the Via tribe departed, leaving the pastures with the cattle, heading toward steadily ascending ground. And I continued to look for any sign of those coins they had stolen from me, as well as my sword.

At least Lily wasn't struggling, for the Via tribe knew where to find water in the Barrens, and from watering hole to watering hole we would go, even as we traveled many miles.

I learned, as I traveled, that the Via tribe was among the greatest tribes in Ardogne. And I learned, from Andeo, that King Diego had been betrayed by his own soldiers, and that he had been driven out of "the City"—Asina Aurea—and had been last seen traveling away on a ship.

A ship… and I presumed that he had taken with him the Briar Rose. The woman Allórie would be upset to hear of it.

And I wondered at the absurdity of the situation I had found myself in… in a foreign land because of Allórie's dark yet bright eyes, because of a feeling and nothing more. "Briar Rose" I said at midday. "Briar Rose," I had said at noon.

And I began to more actively look for my sword, as the caravan continued, swearing I'd cut them all down as soon as it was in my hand. These tribesmen had robbed me; they had intended to kill me. They had done me wrong, even if it was thanks to them that I was alive.

~

The ascent halted at a meadow before one of the low mountains, green grass as tall as my knee, some of which was flowering. And the tribesmen at once, though it was night, began allowing their cattle and lambs to feed. It was a green feast for them, and it was a green feast for Lily, who at once began chewing away.

And though it was dark, as the tents were set up, I looked for an idle chest or a case, a bag or a wicker basket—anything that could carry my sword, and help me deal death to those who had wronged me.

A calf was slaughtered; the stars emerged, and the moon glowed above head. More wine was poured, more meat was eaten, and with it cheese. And I said under my breath, "Briar Rose."

I was in the Barrens in the kingdom called Ardogne, with strange company. And I could not find my sword. It was in their interest that I didn't find it, and I was beginning to suspect they knew it. I was beginning to think that Andeo and Caros and Garo and Labos knew what a deficit there was of trust.

I watched the cattle graze, and under my breath, I said,

"Briar Rose."

~

The stars were out, and I slept outside in a bedroll, not wishing to come into close quarters with the tribesmen. At all hours they smelled of spice and sweat, and I did not think the tribe of Via ever used a washroom, or availed themselves of a swimming hole. My mission was not lost on me—this distraction was not welcome. I was not where I needed to be. I needed to be in Diego's company. I needed to find the Briar Rose.

But why did I need to find the Briar Rose? It was all for a feeling, a compulsion I had felt. That was why—that was why I sought it.

And anew I wondered if the woman Allórie was a sorceress, if, by her powers, she had caused the lightning and the storm to come, and my mind to be filled with idle fancies.

I was now in a different kingdom, in a place that felt like it should be halfway across the world, but was only a few days' ride from the Royal Capital. I had lost track of my goal.

Allórie had promised me the world… her house, ten *libres* in silver. Yet what motivated me was my curiosity.

What was this Briar Rose that a rich woman sought above all else? Did it possess powers of healing? Was it somehow worth much more than her house and ten *libres*? I did not know.

A sound echoed, far off—I looked beyond, and saw what looked at first like a roe buck, but then my eyes focused and my vision cleared… it was a large shaggy goat, its black eyes gleaming, and far off were others, perhaps female goats in his harem, and kids.

I didn't know what was getting into me—another inexplicable feeling had beset me, like when I had agreed to seek after the Briar Rose. I climbed out of my bedroll, and I approached, wondering if goat meat were ever eaten, or if it was considered inedible.

Gingerly, I stooped down; I grabbed a stone in my hand.

And I took off running, sprinting, and the goats began to bound away.

~

What I was doing was inexplicable… perhaps the woman Allórie had cast a spell on me from afar.

I chased the goats through green meadows and beside watering holes, as the ground swiftly ascended. They were quickly outpacing me, and with each stride I made they got away twice as far. The ground began to ascend, at first gradually, then roughly, until I was vaulting myself over a sheer rock face.

And by the time I had climbed the cliff, pulling myself with all my might onto the solid ground, I knew I had lost. I hurled the stone at the vanishing shadows of the goats. And I saw before me was a pool of water, glistening with moonlight. I stooped down and cupped some of the cold water in my hands, and I drank, and I began to regain some of my lost energy.

"You, *grieo*," a woman's voice startled me.

How long had I been sitting here, drinking water, in my underclothes?

Grieo—I understood bits and pieces of their speech. I was not proficient, but I was learning.

I turned around to face her, and there before me was a woman in a long-sleeved red gown, the kind of gown that women of Ardogne seemed to wear. She was beautiful and young, black-haired and black-eyed, and I had seen this woman often in the company of the chieftain Andeo.

Her hair was long, and on her fingers were gold rings.

"You are up late, Lorkdan of Berry Thicket," she said.

"As are you," I said. How long had I been crouching here, sipping water?

"What do you want of me?" I said to her, and I thought I knew.

But her expression suddenly grew grim; her lips twisted into a frown, and her eyes lost their light—they darkened. "I know why my husband brought you here. It is not for your good."

"Will he kill me?" I said.

"No," she said. "He will not—he will do worse. He knows you will not help him. He knows that as soon as you have your sword, you will fight us.

"But there is a tree that grows here, Lorkdan, and its sap… its sap…"

I gazed at her in astonishment, and I wondered why she had betrayed her husband's intent.

Yet more noises were heard, footsteps rustling in the bushes, a storm of them.

A look of panic appeared in the eyes of Andeo's wife. And she rushed downward, down the cliff side, into the meadows and pastureland below.

Warriors were approaching, warriors in white clothing, with curved swords at the ready. I recognized one of them as Andeo's lieutenant.

"What are you doing here, Lorkdan of Berry Thicket?" he said. "Do you intend to escape?"

"If I wanted to escape, you wouldn't be able to stop me," I said.

"Bold," said the lieutenant, "bold, *grieo*. We'll have to tie you up from here on out.

"Come with us!"

And I had no choice.

In the sunlight, we made our move across the meadows. As I traveled, my hands bound in silken cord, I caught Andeo's wife staring at me throughout the day in a way I wasn't sure was appropriate.

The cattle grazed; Lily feasted. The lambs who followed along nibbled at this grassland, blooming in the spring.

And as I walked, the priest joined me, attempting to indoctrinate me in the religion of his god Toro, not knowing that I had pledged myself to the god of the underworld, and to him only did I answer.

"Our god led us here to this valley," he said. "He leads us to all valleys. He caused King Diego to reign in rightness and in justice."

"And did he also cause Jafet to become king?" I said.

I expected a strike, at best some verbal lashing. But instead we continued to walk on, leading the cattle through the grassland as the ground slowly but inevitably ascended.

"Lorkdan, you are proud," said the priest. "You are a Zarube…"

"I am not," I said.

"But you are not of Ardogne. And if you are not a Zarube, then you can see how that kingdom has oppressed all others around it, levying taxes and forcing others to worship their goddess… why then will you not help us?"

"Had I said I would not?" I told him. "I only asked for my sword."

"The wise see your heart," the priest continued. "It is cold and dark, as cold and dark as they come—hardened by much bloodshed. But Toro can soften it."

At his words, I was growing annoyed. Midges were beginning to buzz—I could tell we were approaching water.

More and more, and with greater frequency, I sought out

the case or the bag or whatever hid my sword. And I eyed Lily, who was lagging behind.

A forest appeared ahead.

~

The trees were spindly and grew close together.

My encounter with Andeo's wife I had almost thought a dream. And panic seized me at what they would to do me. My hands were bound; my sword was not in sight. I was stronger than any of them, a man of war, but I was no demigod. I began to panic, but I thought to escape, it would be best to do so in the dark of night.

What did they intend to do to me? The spindly trees were ahead.

As the cattle grazed, the Via tribe began to set up camp. Tents were erected, and I saw a man take out his sitar, another a drum. In the distance, a boy was leading a calf to slaughter.

Andeo's wife and I exchanged glances; there was worry in her eyes, and I couldn't imagine what panic my eyes reflected. Sap, she had told me, sap.

They did not intend to kill me, but instead "worse." What was worse than death? Torture?

I could not begin to imagine.

What was worse to me was being kept in a cage, without my sword—ordered about by people who were not worthy of my respect. What was worse was this—and vainly I stood there, searching about the camp, seeking any sign of my sword. It was my tool, the tool of my trade. It was my pride and joy—and by it, I had overthrown the Count of Valle. I had killed thirty men in the Battle of Ausarne. And these folk of the Via tribe knew what would happen if it fell into my hands again. They were aware all that stood between them and my violent escape was my sword.

The sun was beginning to wane; twilight was falling, and the heat of the day was dwindling. Fireflies were beginning to fly about, brightening and then winking out. The calf that had been slaughtered, now butchered, had been fashioned into slabs of meat that were roasting and steadily dripping their juices into the fire. From the edges of camp, men and women alike were heaving masonry jars where wine was stored.

And in the distance, from the forest, dark shapes were approaching—men, warriors, Andeo. And in Andeo's hand was a bowl.

~

"The sap of the *cara* tree brings vitality," Andeo said. "Vitality, health of body, and vigor. It is an aphrodisiac, some say."

"Why would I have use of *that*?" I said.

"Perhaps, I can find a manner in which an aphrodisiac will be useful for you," Andeo said.

I eyed his wife, but wondered what other tribal woman he had in mind.

Instead I looked at him, and spoke in a tone that gave no space for disagreement. "I will not drink the *cara* sap, Andeo," I said. "I will not, and if you wish to feed it to me, you'll have to force it down my mouth. May Toro help you if you are foolish enough to try that."

"So little trust," Andeo said. "So little trust."

What was worse than death? I supposed it was this—this situation I was in, having lost my freedom, having lost my sword. Was this drink of sap somehow worse? I couldn't imagine.

"Tonight you will feast," Andeo said, "and you will learn to trust."

My binds were loosened. Music began to play, a flute, a

drum. Before me was set a wooden platter, on which was a slab of tender beef, red in the center, smeared in salt. My mouth watered, but I wondered if in the Via tribe's craftiness they had smeared the sap of the *cara* tree onto it. I took the beef, licked it, and tasted nothing strange, and so—with the spoon and knife set before me, I took to my meal.

A tall glass of wine was slammed onto my platter and my mouth felt dry at the sight of it, but I wanted to keep my wits about me in such a dangerous place, in such an uncertain situation, amid such dangerous company.

But the music, and the night, was filling my mind, and by the time I'd finished my giant slab of meat, the heavy salt had caused me to thirst. I searched for the sight of water—but nothing was in view. And the wine, mixed with honey, reminded me so much of a tall glass of ale.

A woman in a crimson dress came twirling by, dancing to the music. And I grabbed my goblet of wine, and I drank—first one sip, then two.

~

I had finished the glass when a beautiful Via maiden came by, and with a jug filled my glass to the brim. I knew I had to keep my wits about me—but two surely wouldn't affect my judgment.

I set it down—it was filled again, and in that moment I realized I was the only person drinking… the last cogent thought I'd have of the night.

Another drink… another drink… my mind was swimming, and I was beginning to feel dizzy. Even sitting in a chair, I thought I might fall. In the distance were the concerned eyes of Andeo's wife—but what was she worried about?

Another drink… another… I caught a reflection of myself

in one of the warrior's shields, and my once pearly white teeth were stained purple. I did not care… I wanted another drink.

And at last, bewildered, staggered, confused, I saw that the people of the Via tribe were gathered around me, and Andeo was standing there, proffering a bowl in his hands. What was that bowl?

"What is that bowl?" I said.

"It is medicine for your bones," Andeo said. "Fire for your blood… eagerness for your heart. Drink it and it will transform you into something new!"

It sounded like a good proposition… but hadn't I been afraid of something, before I began to drink? Hadn't I been afraid of something—indeed, terrified?

But the bowl was pressed to my lips, and the taste was sickly sweet, like syrup. I began to cough—to choke. I struggled, and I fell backward in my chair.

~

My mind was swimming, and I felt my world was swaying to this side and then the other. Up above me were stars. Andeo was hovering above me… Andeo…

But his face was changing, and it looked like that of a bull. Two piercing eyes, and a voice, and I knew whatever he said was the law.

"You will overthrow Jafet, Lorkdan of Berry Thicket. It is my command—the command of Toro, god of Ardogne.

"You will overthrow Jafet, like you overthrew the Count of Valle, and you will place his brother Diego on the throne."

"I will," I said—and I would. Now I was convinced, possessed of zeal. I pictured in my mind Jafet… I pictured in my mind tossing him off the throne with my bare hands.

"I will," I said—and I would.

The luminous figure grabbed my hands, and lifted me to my feet.

"Here, Lorkdan," the luminous figure said, "your sword."

My sword was placed into my hands, and new energy filled me.

Chapter Thirteen:
The Task

In the morning, I woke. The sun was shining, and the wind was wafting through meadows. I was eager to go about my task, eager to tear the false king Jafet from his throne.

I had a splitting headache—had I drunk wine? I could remember hardly anything from last night.

But the leader of the Via tribe was walking toward me. My sword was in its sheath. And I was possessed in that moment by an overwhelming urge to finish this quest. Jafet was in my sights; and it was my life's purpose—it was my life's goal to overthrow him.

"Where," I said, "where is Lily?"

One of the boys of the Via tribe was leading my donkey by the reins to me.

"Where," I said, "is Jafet? I will kill him! I will kill him!"

Andeo had begun to smile, but his wife was drawing near me, and when she looked at me it was in pity. Why would she pity me? Why would she pity me—I, in the prime of my life, ready to set about my most important task? I, Lorkdan of Berry Thicket, would be the one to destroy the false king Jafet—I would tear him from his kingship, and set his brother on the throne.

"Jafet is in the City," Andeo said.

"Asina Aurea," I said.

"That is what outsiders call it," Andeo replied.

The boy brought Lily to me; I hopped astride her.

"Where is Asina Aurea? What is the way?" I said.

"You will find it," said Andeo, "when you seek it."

In his hand, there appeared a flaming brand; he struck Lily, and she brayed harshly, and took off, across the meadows, in the rising sun.

~

Past the meadows, we were in the Barrens again. My belt felt heavy; I touched at it, and felt fabric. I looked; and there was my coin purse. They had given me back my coin purse—why?

But it was not as weighty as it had been.

Sand and dust greeted me, a harsh blazing sun and withering heat. The only greenness were the thorny plants that clung to life in these hellish plains—the only feature that stood out were the low mountains which contained no water.

I was back where I had begun, but a new fire consumed me. I would tear Jafet down from his throne—and I would make his brother king.

Part Four

There I was, back again, in the desert land called the Barrens, wandering, unaware of what had been done to me, or what poison I had drunk.

—Lorkdar, "Records from Evre Prison"

Chapter Fourteen: City of Wonders

The air ahead of me wavered; the sun's heat was choking. When I breathed, I coughed at the dust, and small particles were stinging my eyes.

I was growing thirsty—my waterskin was nigh empty. But this time, I was convinced of my mission, passionate... to find Asina Aurea, and deal death to the false king who ruled over it.

As morning turned to noon and noon to midday, small watering holes began to appear amid the dust and sand, around which were growing grasses and palmetto trees. Birds more and more circled overhead, eagles and hawks and doves, but above all vultures with red faces, their bodies cloaked in black feathers.

In the distance were the bones of a giant ox—the remnants of a wagon, and I thought of pilfering it.

Instead, I coaxed Lily on, despite her complaints, as the sand turned to dust and the dust to dirt.

We began to ascend a rocky ridge, a low hill, and mountains were before me, and mountains were beside me. There were bubbling pools, and then at last a road, appearing out of nowhere— the road I had first seen when I entered this accursed country, which had disappeared into the dust. Something else reached my nose—the smell of filth. I caught my first glimpse of people suddenly, dozens of men wandering about the way.

The road began to wind up a steep hill, and amid the heat, Lily was panting and heaving. Crowds now swarmed about me on either side, men in long tunics and women in red dresses. The hill peaked, and there, far below me, beside the glittering sea, was a city of immense size—a gleaming wonder by the shore.

Its walls were colored like gold, each brick the size of an oxcart, perfectly fitted so that it almost seemed hewn from one rock. At its walls were four gates, one leading out to the sea and the harbor, in which there were ships of many-colored sails; another led north, to a place of farms; another east, facing the mountain. One gate was before me, at the bottom of this hill. I was in the town of Asina Aurea, and my entry was not guaranteed.

My heart seized up at the sight of it, at first in wonder, then in fear.

The buildings stretched into the horizon, flat roofed and made from bright-white plaster, built on many sloping hills. I scanned for any sign of the palace wherein my enemy lay, the king of Ardogne—Jafet. In the east of the city was a mighty building hewn of stone, of the same make as the walls. Its towers and turrets had many crenellations, and were decorated throughout with small black bits of metalwork. Time had turned the stone of that castle darker, and now it was not colored gold, but ochre, near red.

I could tell this city was alive—alive, like the Royal City had been, before the famine and the hunger swept across the land. There were no signs of such trouble in the city before me. The seas were filled with ships—not just sleek ships of Ardogne but ships with lateen sales and even dhows sailing this way and that, bearing merchandise to Asina Aurea.

I coaxed Lily, and her resistance was broken after a few kicks. The road swiftly descended, and I in my Zarube dress had never felt so foreign and out of place.

I was drawing near—but the sun was growing low in the sky, and I knew that soon the gate would shut.

~

At the gate were soldiers, men in suits of mail and iron

helmets, with scimitars and shields, on which were painted lion motifs. They were letting the men and women of Ardogne pass by, but as I drew near, they began to shout in their foreign tongue.

"You! *Grieo!*" one said.

I began to assume the word meant "foreigner."

"What are you doing?" he said—the chief of them, it seemed, for on his helmet was a gold marking. "You are not allowed. No *grieos* are allowed in Asina Aurea. What is the meaning of this?"

No one ever accused me of wittiness—no one ever said I was clever or crafty. But I tried to think of something to say, some pretense to pass through the gate. Amid my stammering and my indecision, he drew near me. Soon, he was just feet away.

"You are bearing a sword," he said. "Are you a vagrant? A bandit? A thief?"

It dawned on me that I had seen no civilian walking into Asina Aurea with a weapon at his side. In the Royal City, many had a dagger at the ready, a cane or even a sword like mine. To not have one was a mark of poverty.

Ah, I had been a fool to barge in so recklessly, to not have had a plan.

"Southrons we welcome," said the chief guard. "Ariaks too. But Zarubes are the worst of foreigners; you will not pass through these gates."

"I am not a Zarube," I said, "I am of the East—far East."

"Pale, dull, blue eyes, hulking brutes… you are the same," said the chief guard. "You look like a Zarube to me. Begone."

The sun was beginning to set, and the scattered Ardognian passersby were hurrying through the gate as it ground close.

I walked off, considering, praying under my breath, hoping for some miracle of the god of the underworld I worshipped, but in my heart I felt it would not come.

The trees outside the city of Asina Aurea were far apart, and consisted of pines and palms, hugging the shore. The air quickly grew cool, losing all its heat, until I was shivering and felt colder than I ever had in Zarubad, the Royal City. I was in the darkness, plotting, thinking, underneath the vault of the stars. I dismounted from Lily and let her chew at the scattered grasses, though they did not cover all of the dusty ground, and in places, there was sand.

As I walked amid the dry ground, I found myself at last leaning against a palm tree. Its bark was coarse against my hand.

And visions began to return, a light-wreathed figure, a being—and a command. He had said that the god Toro demanded I unseat the false king Jafet.

But my quarry was in the city… my prey was beyond those walls.

How could I get in? I was not one to connive, not one to deceive or disguise my intentions. Some would say I wasn't smart enough; I said I was too honorable. My sword was my tool; it was an extension of my hand. My tool was not cunning words and disguised intentions.

I could fight my way in… cut down the guards, but even I, Lorkdan, could not overcome an entire army; the king of Ardogne could deal death to me, if he focused all his might, and sent all his soldiers after me.

I had been denied entry—but I was beginning to remember words, half-forgotten, that the god of Ardogne lived on a mountain near the city.

It was preposterous, I knew, for the gods lived in heaven, but I could see the dark outline of a great mountain right before me, one of those low purplish mountains like I had seen in the Barrens. The god Toro lived on that mountain, it was said—the mountain just outside the city.

And an inexplicable feeling took me towards it. I grabbed

Lily by the reins and led her for a while, then at last mounted her. I drove her on; and she did not put up much resistance. I rode her toward the mountain into the deepening night.

Chapter Fifteen: The Temple

In the dark there were scattered lights—the light of a torch, and of a lantern. Nevertheless, I pressed on, knowing my chances of detection were small, and that the mountain north of the city was scarcely inhabited.

As I drew near to the slope, the ground began to ascend, first slowly, then quickly, until at last there were sheer rock walls that I could not climb, and where Lily could not go. But the lights of the torches far below me lit up small portions of the ground. And I could see a staircase in the distance, far ahead, carved into the mountain, with steps small enough for Lily to navigate.

I coaxed her on, and she needed little encouragement.

I knew I was taking a great risk, but my curiosity was piqued.

~

On Lily, I traversed the steps, and the further I traveled, the brisker and colder the night air grew, and the harsher were the blowing winds. Soon, the slightest gust was like a dagger to my neck.

Statues of bulls and cows were beginning to greet me, bulls and cows standing on two feet like humans, some with moon crowns on their heads. And I knew I was beginning to enter what was considered by those of Ardogne a sacred place, and by virtue of that, I was headed into danger. If they didn't allow *grieos* into their City, would they allow them into their temple?

Up I traveled; the skies darkened. The moon and stars were cloaked. There was a rain, at first misting, then a downpour. And the steps of the staircase began to grow slick.

Amid the harsh rain, I continued on, following a feeling

inexplicable, like I had so many times before.

I had first traveled to Ardogne for a reason other than Jafet… but I couldn't remember why. But when I thought of it, I thought of dark eyes, luscious lips, and the picture of a rose.

Lily began to struggle, and though she never lost her footing, I did not feel quite comfortable riding on her. As the rain poured down, I dismounted and began to lead her along, but she brayed, and she resisted.

"Suit yourself," I said, and I knew she'd remain in place.

On my feet, in my boots, I traveled upwards, and to the rain was added the sound of far-off thunder. The air became cold, and I thought it might snow, but the rain was strangely hot against my skin.

The stairs ended their ascent; in the rain were two dusky faces, men in armor, bearing scimitars and swords.

"*Grieo! Grieo!*" they cried, and gave me no chance to offer a defense. They charged me with their swords, struck; I drew mine, and in two strokes they were dead, one beheaded, one impaled.

They fell bleeding to the ground and again there was the far-off rumble of thunder.

~

I was at the summit of the mountain, and the rain ceased suddenly; the downpour had stopped as suddenly as it started, but the flagstone remained wet.

There were torches ahead, scattered voices. I was alone in this holy place; and I was sure that I had defiled it.

Yet I was not one to back down; I drew near. There was a great brazier, the circumference of a house, which was now smoldering and giving off steam. And I saw that the flagstone I walked on was etched in chalk with many markings and runes.

When I looked ahead, as my eyes adjusted, I could see what the night darkness had conspired to hide—a building of stone with a pyramidal red roof, and a door that was opened, standing before it many guards.

But when I walked ahead there was a shout; a guard ran, and that set off a frenzy—they all began to sprint away. One was foolish enough to stand there in his bravado, alone, until I rattled my sword, and he ran off.

I was venturing into the temple. Why was I doing it? I did not know.

~

The darkness in the temple was deep. I could see there were several ceremonial rooms, in which there were assorted cult objects—a striped cloth of cotton, a doll, and several unlit braziers.

My feelings had led me here, but I was sure in the eyes of those of Ardogne I was committing the utmost sacrilege. I, a *grieo*, was in this place.

I walked on and knocked over a gold object. I stumbled, almost tripped, and bowled over a pot, which collapsed into shards.

Why was I here? I did not know. It was a feeling, and of late I'd been given to feelings.

Light appeared in the distance, light shining through a bronze door.

What was behind that bronze door? I drew up to it, and saw that there were handles. I took the handle in my hand, and yanked it open.

Before me was a room lit by gold lanterns, on a chair a man wearing a bull's skin. At once, he stood up and for a moment he was silent; then he began to shout. Through the bull's skin covering his mouth I could not understand a word.

There was a spear next to him; I only noticed it when he picked it up. He grabbed it by the haft and heaved it toward me; he struck at me, I parried.

One stroke of my sword and he was dead, beheaded.

In his room were glittering gold objets d'art, a table of marble, paintings, teak chairs and a desk on which was a platter, covered in half-eaten foods. I was getting ready to loot the room when shouts appeared behind; I had company.

~

In the front vestibule of the temple were warriors bearing torches, garbed in mail. The look in their eyes when they saw me was disbelief. My sword was dripping fresh blood.

I was in the dark; they could scarcely make out my form. I dashed ahead, struck one down, and then took off, sprinting, into the outside air, under the stars and moon. The sweet smell of flowers greeted me.

Chapter Sixteen: Tabula

Sheltering under a pine from the day's heat, with Lily close beside, I could see the smoke of many fires rising up above the walls of Asina Aurea, dark black plumes against the blue sky. The morning I had spent hiding away, for fear I'd been seen in the mountain temple.

But the smoke was growing, and even from where I stood, I could hear shouts, and the far-off clang of metal. The gates of the city were shut, and they had been shut all morning.

Crowds of would-be entrants, natives all, had gathered outside the gate and been told to remain outside. I eyed the wall and saw that, unlike yesterday, there were no guards posted on the battlements—no person in sight. The bricks of the wall from a distance had seemed uniform, but so close I could see there were possible handholds.

Could I climb the wall and enter the city? Would I face certain death?

And if I climbed into Asina Aurea, where would I keep Lily?

No—it was best to wait.

Unbidden, I ventured to the gate, seeing the crowds gathered there, the spurned travelers. I looked up to the mountain and in the daylight saw the steps, which now were filled with soldiers.

I spoke to those gathered at the gate, and they told me a riot had started—they did not know why, and no one was allowed to enter or to leave until the "ruffians" were dealt with. I looked to the shores of the sea.

If I swam into the harbor, perhaps I could enter. Perhaps, the guards would not notice me. But a *grieo* would stick out like a sore thumb. Perhaps, I should wait. But this riot that had started had provided an opportunity.

Again, I looked to the walls. The bricks seemed easy to scale. Was I so daring? Was I so foolish? And what about Lily?

Fortune was with those who acted swiftly, who feared not. I grabbed hold of one of the bricks, and then another. I almost fell. But I climbed.

Slowly, steadily, I made my ascent, but halfway up, the wall shuddered and I fell.

Bruised, broken, the wind knocked from my lungs, I was reeling, my mind swimming—and when my vision cleared, I saw that the gate had been burst open, and a motley mob was pouring out of the city, sprinting toward the mountain steps, toward the temple which I had so severely defiled last night.

As they ran, I slipped in at first among them, then pushed on, through the open gate, into the city proper.

~

The streets were narrow, little better than alleys, dry and dusty.

Under the sun, the air was dry, and the quality of that air was poor.

The sounds of battle were further off—the mob had escaped, but more fires were beginning to burn. I looked ahead, and even from where I stood I could see the stone castle with its crenellated towers. That was where I should go—it was where the false king Jafet no doubt was. Yet again I followed a feeling, but this feeling was now accompanied by a thought—I had found my way into the city. I should find a place to hide. Where best was there in such a city for a *grieo* to hide?

Seagulls circled overhead—I had my answer.

~

In the harbor was less chaos and pandemonium. Indeed, commerce continued, and amid the docks and wharfs, the ships and the gleaming dinghies in the sea, the crowds cloaked me. Fishermen were dressing their catch of the day on tables. Ox carts were carrying loads of crates or barrels into the city proper.

But I still stood out in my Zarube dress, my tunic and my trousers and my sword. In the day's light I heard some begin to shout—suspicious eyes greeted me. I hurried on my way.

~

I navigated the rabbit's warren of city streets. In every neighborhood and borough, clotheslines hung from upper story window to upper story window. I felt I was being followed, but I was making no progress. In such a city as this, I stuck out, by my clothing, by my very appearance.

In the distance I heard a call, "*Grieo! Grieo!*"

I looked back to see a gang of natives running toward me.

I turned down an alley and saw a darkened door. I knew nowhere else to hide. I ran into it.

~

Darkness indeed hid me. There was the light of candles but that light was faint. There were a few people sitting in chairs and tables, but they couldn't see me clearly. To them, I was just a dark form—tall and muscular, and with a sword at my side, but only a dark shape.

I was in a tavern and the tables were of fine dark wood, overlaid with rich silken cloths. The floor was of smooth stone and swept clean.

Amid the darkness a graceful shadow began to approach. Two eyes twinkled in the candlelight.

"*Grieo*," she said, and my heart seized up. "I thought the guards did not let your kind into the city… ever since King Jafet assumed power, it has been so."

Grieo—not all had such enmity toward us.

But through the doorway others were emerging, men with knives—those following me.

"*Grieo! Grieo!*" they said.

But the woman called out, "Will you spill blood in a *tabula*?"

And they grimaced, and their anger seemed to grow, but they stepped backward and their strength seemed to wither, and they turned and ran outside.

"Jafet brings out the worst in us," said the woman, the barkeep of this *tabula*—tavern.

And it seemed that in Ardogne, a tavern was a place where blood was not to be shed. In the Royal City, it was the opposite.

"Who are you?" I said to the woman.

"I am Yacinda," she said. "I just saved your life."

"It would seem that way," I said. "How much for a room? A bit of food? Perhaps, something to slake my thirst…"

"For a *grieo*, free," Yacinda said. "I haven't seen any of your kind since Jafet took over. And I think it is a pity.

"Call me a doer of good deeds, a patron of the lost… you are lucky to have survived these streets. Jafet's thugs are running rampant, and it seems nothing can stop them. At least, until last night…"

"What happened last night?" I said.

"Our 'god' was killed," Yacinda said. "Hurry, hide yourself in the shadows. I will have my kitchen crew fashion you something to eat."

Their "god" was killed. Toro. I had killed Toro. I wondered what Andeo would say.

~

I took a seat in the dark corners of the room, and the darkness hid my face, my *grieo* appearance and physique. The *tabula* or tavern, which I learned was called The Crimson Cup, was not well populated, and few seemed to patronize it. That was good for me, but not good, I suppose, for Yacinda and for those who worked under her.

My stomach was growling; my tongue felt dry. I became aware of a spicy aroma that stung my eyes, the scent of cooking meat and dough, and the tantalizing sound of wine chugging into a goblet. It was brought to me, carried by two serving girls — a platter of silver, and on that platter, an assortment of plates.

Some were of steamed dumplings; others were roasted bits of meat, or assemblies of steamed vegetables lathed in butter — pork rinds, and mashed tubers, all coated in a layer of red-hot spice. A third serving girl set before me a goblet of wine, the largest wine-goblet I'd ever seen.

And I realized that Ardogne was not suffering from the famine.

And I thought of something my mother had taught me — "Nothing is ever free."

And I remembered Yacinda's words, of what had occurred last night. I had sparked those riots — the mob storming its way to the temple. All that had been done by my own sword.

I began to pick apart the various foods, with my fingers, for

I had been provided no fork or knife. I began to eat, and my eyes watered at the spices, and my tongue began to burn, but plate by plate I was growing full, after so long eating little at all, mostly water.

Yacinda was staring at me from a dark corner. *Grieo*, she called me. She wanted to protect me. Why?

By the time I was finished, and my watering eyes had begun to dribble tears, and I was sipping at my wine for relief, she was drawing near me. I had so many questions of this Madame Yacinda, so many questions that needed answering, which I wasn't sure I'd be provided.

She sat down next to me. "How did you like it?" she said.

"Very good," I said, "but as I ate it, I remembered something my mother said — 'nothing is ever free.'"

"Your mother is right, *grieo*," Yacinda said.

I continued to sip my wine. "And what do you want?"

There was a commotion up ahead, near the door. Yacinda panicked, grabbed me by the hand, almost launched me across the room, to the cellar door — and I understood her instructions intuitively. Doing my best to disguise all sound, I hurried into the cellar darkness, and hid between two oak barrels, as shouted voices reached me from up above.

"We hear you are hiding an intruder in your establishment, Yacinda!" said one of the voices. "One of the Red Guards said so."

"I am a *pereto*!" I heard Yacinda say. "A lover of the king and crown… loyal to Jafet. The Red Guards don't seem to be recruiting the best anymore."

"Shall we look?" said another shouted voice. And I slid my sword underneath one of the barrels, and, stretching my limbs, bending and twisting and struggling, climbed underneath the other, perfectly hidden.

Footsteps echoed above head, more scattered shouts I could not distinguish, and icy sweat was beginning to form on my arms, and wet my eyes. The darkness cloaked me — the darkness, and a barrel. But I feared my sword was out of place.

Too late — the cellar door opened, a man began to descend and scour the room, with a candle. I remained perfectly still and stopped my breathing.

Footsteps echoed — above me and beside.

But after he had searched the cellar, he turned and walked up the steps. "No one is in there!" I heard him say from above.

I thanked the stars — I thanked Balzor god of the underworld. I waited, until the footsteps echoed, and more scattering murmurs greeted me, then vanished into silence. The cellar door opened, and I smelled Yacinda's perfume.

I stood up, and saw her bright eyes twinkle. Her grin was a balm to my soul.

"They are gone, Jafet's thugs — you are safe."

~

I was led through this tabula, or rather *tavern*, through the main hall, down a side corridor to where the light of the sun shone through glass windows. I was being led into the interior of this tavern called The Crimson Cup, where there were marble floors. I was taken to the parlor, where red divans surrounded a crystal table, and on that table a game of backgammon. Green plants in pots were growing in this room, so bright it was like a solarium. And I knew I did not need to hide.

"When have you last bathed?" said Yacinda.

I could see she was dusky like the others of Ardogne, that her hair was a raven black, her lips red and luscious. Her eyes though were fair, and the red dress she wore unlike the others I'd seen was made of the finest materials, perhaps some mixture of silk.

"I did not think those of Ardogne favored bathing," I said.

"I hadn't seen it until now. The Via tribe — "

"The tribesmen," Yacinda said, and she seemed amused. "Our unruly cousins. They do not bathe, or many things that the city people do. Jafet wants to civilize them — a fool's task."

It was my goal to overthrow Jafet, though I did not remember why.

"So he has declared war on them, driving them from their meadows and their pasturelands," Yacinda said. "Those he captures he brings back to the City... indoctrinates them. Tries to civilize a people who can never be civilized. One more strike against Jafet.

"He is not the legal king. But he had supporters in the army, and supporters in the streets. The Red Guards have terrorized our city for a long time, but only last year did their efforts come to fruition. The generals turned against Diego. And it was all over for him then. But now there is hope."

"Why hope?" I said.

"Our 'god' Toro has been killed — and Jafet couldn't hide the news. The watchers of the Eternal Fire were driven away by a 'phantom' — and the rains were allowed to squelch it. A terrible portent, and now the people are angry... they are angry that Jafet ever allowed it to come to this.

"The Eternal Fire determined the fate of Ardogne. As long as its fire was kept, the nation would prevail. But a 'phantom' caused the watchers to flee."

I was that phantom — I was the one who had caused all this. And I wasn't sure how I felt about it.

"Cowards all — a man with a sword, or a phantom. A living being or a ghost. In the eyes of the superstitious, they destroyed Ardogne.

"King Jafet tried mightily to hide this fact. He reestablished the fires in the morning — found someone new to play Toro. But we of the City are loose lipped and word spreads from house to house, tongue to tongue. Nothing can be hidden, every dark deed is spoken of in every house and tavern. Nothing can be kept quiet."

"Nothing," I said, "nothing can — in Asina Aurea."

That was what it seemed.

As I looked at Yacinda, I anew began to be suspicious. Her bright eyes twinkled as I spoke. "Nothing is free, my mother said. What is your price?"

"I rather like *grieos*," said Yacinda, "I like them best of all."

To the twinkle in her eyes was added the gleam of lust. She touched my hand with hers. She was beautiful, in a way.

~

When we made love, I was reminded of something, a forgotten memory buried somewhere deep in my mind. I thought of dark eyes that were strangely bright, the image of a rose but that rose was forged of gold, and its blossom was brighter than any rose I'd seen. Thorns had been crafted along its stem.

But amid our passion, my mission did not leave my mind. When at last exhausted we began to fall asleep, my lips uttered the words "Briar Rose" — why? But my mind was focused… Jafet, his brother. An impostor on the throne.

Exhausted, I fell asleep, my fingers running through Yacinda's dark hair.

~

The light of dawn stirred me up. Yacinda was just awake.

I was next to her — and I was looking at her in a new way. To say I trusted her was too bold a statement, but we had been brought close. We were sprawled across the bed, and I said to her under the breath, "I'm here for a purpose, you know. A *grieo* in a city where I can hardly speak the language."

"You struggle," said Yacinda, "but you seem to understand it."

"Aye. I do."

"And why have you come?" said Yacinda.

"To overthrow Jafet," I said, "and place his brother Diego on the throne."

"By yourself?" Yacinda said, and her eyes twinkled once more, and the lust seemed to have returned. "By yourself? You think so highly of yourself, ah…

"I have made love to you, *grieo,* but I do not know your name."

"Lorkdan," I said.

"Lorkdan—of Berry Thicket? The one who overthrew the Count of Valle?"

Was there any place on this earth where my name was not known, where my exploits had not been told of?

The lust in her eyes seemed to grow even more. Gingerly she stroked my whiskers. "Lorkdan," she said, "of Berry Thicket. You are Ardogne's best hope.

"But even you cannot overcome all the king's bodyguard, the Red Guards who patrol the streets… the corrupt generals, the soldiers, the armies."

"Do you think so little of me?" I said.

"I think the world of you," said Yacinda, "and you know that.

"But you are going about this all wrong. If you intend to overthrow the king of Ardogne, you can't just barge in. You must have help — and you are a *grieo.* You will be killed on sight."

"Then what would you have me do, my love?" I said.

Yacinda seemed tickled by my words. Her pearly white grin turned to a smile, and she stroked my whiskers again.

"I'll tell you, Lorkdan, soon enough," she said.

And she laid her hand on my arm.

~

In the dark of the tavern, my face and features hidden, a breakfast was prepared for me — like dinner ferried on a great platter, on which were small plates. On one plate were fresh berries, on another a bowl of sweet pudding, on another a piece of layered cake, and the last a syrupy drink made from those green desert plants. I was being well fed, and for free — and the task I'd been given in exchange for housing and food was not difficult at all. But it was not my chief task; it was not my ultimate mission. That would come later.

When I finished the small plates, I feared I wouldn't have any appetite for later in the day, but I supposed that was just as well. I had a king to overthrow — a rebellion to plan. And Yacinda had promised to offer me her most cogent advice.

Throughout the morning, more patrons would filter in, and I eyed them suspiciously at all hours, wondering if they were loyalists of Jafet—members of the street mob that Yacinda had called the Red Guard.

But the tavern was dark and ill lit, and the candles did not provide much light. It seemed there was an unwritten code among those gathered there that everyone mind their own business, to not inquire of others what they were doing and what tasks they had set about. It was the perfect place for revolutionaries, but If I had to guess, I'd say I was the only revolutionary in the room.

A serving girl took the silver platter; another came by with a steaming drink—tea it smelled like, but darker, and when I held the porcelain cup up to my lips and sipped, it was bitter.

Yacinda emerged from the darkness of the room. She was

holding something—a candle, and a small canvas bundle. She set the candle down, and then spread out the bundle—it was a map, of Ardogne, crudely drawn. In one place in the far west of the peninsula called Ardogne was a dark mark and the words *Asina Aurea.*

"You need help," said Yacinda, "and to offer you help in this some would call treason." She was almost speaking at a whisper. "But Jafet's reign has been terror… the Red Guards marching through the streets, committing crimes without fear of prosecution. The tribesmen persecuted and scattered. Living in fear of his edicts. Not long ago the king feared the people; but now it is the opposite."

I had come to Asina Aurea to overthrow the king Jafet—but I could not remember why. I was not given to pity stories, but this task had been imprinted on my mind—why? Who had given it to me? I remembered a light-wreathed figure, and I felt the burning desire in my heart.

"King Diego sailed away just in time, before the Red Guards could tear him limb from limb. He is hiding somewhere in the Numinous Isles off the shore. You must seek his help. You cannot do it alone, Lorkdan."

I felt challenged. I did not like to be doubted. "Watch me," I said.

~

For the first time in a long time, I was in the brightness of the sun, and the sun's heat was beating harshly down upon me. Clouds were wisping by in the blue sky. The air was dry and dusty and poor in quality.

"*Grieo! Grieo!*" A child was shouting the insult—and he was pointing at me down the street.

Adults soon caught wind of me, men in long tunics, several with knives. And they began to shout and chase after me, and I ran.

I darted through alleyways and streets, underneath clotheslines, beside wicker baskets and crates. I was trying to lose my attackers, but every street I turned down, more people noticed me and began to cry *"Grieo! Grieo!"*

Mobs were following me, men and women, some with crimson scarfs around their necks—presumably Red Guards. But I was faster than them, yes faster. And though I zigzagged through the city, winding through the labyrinth of streets, I had always in my mind the great castle that loomed above the city, built of reddish stone, its crenellated towers taller than the towers of the king's castle back in the Royal City.

I shoved past men and women and children alike, spilling the wicker baskets they carried on their heads. I leapt over carts filled with melons and fruit, and pushed past snarling wild dogs.

The Royal Castle was drawing nearer—but arrows were beginning to fly. The rude mob had acquired bows, or crossbows, making my task all that much harder.

A plaza opened up before me, staggering in size—a plaza of red-brick stone underneath the sky the size of many fields, at the head of which was a wall, and beyond that wall Asina Aurea's castle.

And before that wall was an angry mob, thousands strong, filling half the plaza. People were trying to scale the wall, climbing from handhold to handhold. I could hear scattered chants about Jafet and about Toro and about "the Eternal Fire."

I unsheathed my sword and sprinted toward the mob, even as more arrows flew, but failed to strike me.

~

In the mob I was cloaked by their bodies, disguised by

virtue of their presence, by virtue of their anger. Their angry shouts rose up into the heat of the day. They were angry about what King Jafet had allowed to be done—but it was the *grieo* standing among them that had done it.

"Go! Go!" I shouted in their tongue, encouraging the rabble vaulting over bricks and stones, even as Jafet's soldiers poured pots of boiling water on them or jabbed them with spears. They were unarmed, they were poor—they were rabble, but they were numerous, outnumbering the king's soldiers by multitudes. I had come to them in the heat of the moment, but if they cared I was a *grieo* they showed no sign of it.

"Here," a woman said, bright eyed and fairly-complected. She handed me a stone. I laughed at the sight of it, but in one hand I took it, and I hurled it at one of the guards on the walls.

"Toro! Toro!" the voices rose up. "É Toro!"

A member of the mob managed to scale the wall, but he was cut down.

But noise erupted behind—and the triumphant shouts of the mob withered into fear. Trumpets were blowing; the mob was surrounded. Soldiers were moving in, men in chainmail with sparkling helms, in their hands spears and swords. There were hundreds—they were outnumbered by the mob, but the mob was greatly outmatched.

I ran to the wall, laid my handholds on the bricks, wondering if this would be the day that I, Lorkdan, died. With my sword in one hand and my other free to climb, I began to launch myself upwards, but the footholds were poor, and twice I slipped, until at last I crashed to the ground. The soldiers were cutting down the mob—it seemed that King Jafet did not honor the lives of his subjects.

But I rallied the mob, shouted at the top of my lungs, "Fight! For Toro!"

And galvanized by the *grieo* standing next to them, they seemed to be filled with zeal, and with what weapons they had began to charge at Jafet's soldiers, with clubs, with knives, with daggers and some with stolen swords. The soldiers cut down the mob swiftly, but when I charged forth and met them, some gasped and terror, and one fell back.

I parried a soldier's spear with my sword; I plunged my blade through his chest. I barreled through more of them, engaging three at once. And the mob met me in their strength of numbers. I had bought them a chance. But their chances remained poor. Two lay bleeding at my hand, then a third. But one swiped me with the butt end of his spear, beating me across the jaw, and drew blood.

The soldiers were cutting the mob down ruthlessly, slaying these citizens of Ardogne without a thought of their rights. But I supposed in Ardogne, and in the west in general, the common were not afforded many rights. It was not a free place like my home, and I pitied these people.

I cut a soldier down; another was bleeding at my feet. But the soldiers were pressing in, mowing down the mob.

Liberty was dying in Asina Aurea... what little flame of liberty had existed before was being snuffed out.

And I realized that I, Lorkdan, could not contend with all these armed men.

Fortune favored boldness; but I had been too bold. I turned to look at the wall, to what I had sought in vain... the overthrow of the king, I in my boldness trying to do what I had done before in Valle. But the gods were not with me; Balzor, god of the underworld, did not favor me. It was not so. As blood dripped onto the stones of the square, and I began to feel faint, I was drawing backwards, no longer on offense but vainly batting away the spear strikes of Jafet's men.

A spear cut me on the cheek; another grazed my arm.

And soon the mob had turned and dissipated, and only I was standing there.

"*Grieo*," said one of the soldiers, who I recognized as the man I'd seen in the gate. "Lorkdan. The underworld's champion. Unhand your sword."

Chapter Seventeen: The Rebel King

The dungeon of the Castle Ambra was dark, and my hands were tied with manacles. It was like the dark of night, if in such a night there were no moon or stars. I wondered what Jafet's men had in store for me, if they would boil me alive or turn me into a mince, if they would burn me at the stake in view of the people, on the great plaza that faced the castle. What would Jafet do if he knew that I, Lorkdan, had joined in with those who had tried overthrow him? His cruelty to his own people was unthinkable; what would it be for a *grieo*, a foreigner, whom it seemed all of Ardogne despised—all save Yacinda who loved them.

I tried the manacles, though I knew it was a fool's task. The harsh metal caused my arms to bleed, and I felt famished and spent.

But a light was glowing, drawing near like a will-o-wisp, and I heard scattered complaints from the inmates. The light drew near until it was blazing in my face, near blinding me—a lantern, that was what it was. "Lorkdan," said the soldier from before, the one I'd seen at the city gate. "Your trial is ahead."

A trial—and what sort of trial could I expect in a foreign land? I, a *grieo*. And I had committed an act of rebellion—in all kingdoms, the sentence was death. They would try to fashion something worse for me than death, torture, burning, pain—but I considered that nothing compared to this, being kept in a cage.

With a set of keys, he unlocked my manacles. I stood up, dizzy. Other soldiers appeared; my wrists were cinched in rope. And I was led up a slick stone stairwell, into a place of light.

~

The throne room of Castle Ambra stole my breath. Throughout a vast room of green and blue tiles, beneath a skylight that let in richly the light of the sun, beside rows of pointed arches that surrounded either side of the chamber, I was led. The room smelled of incense and curry and spice. The throne was forged of pure gold, lined in diamonds, and the man who sat upon it wore a checkered green robe. On his head was a gold crown studded with emerald, ruby and jasper.

He was dusky like others of Ardogne—young for a king, and thin. In his left hand was a scepter, forged of electrum, topped in sapphire. In this place, he had made his cruel decrees. And amid the opulence, the marvels of architecture that were intended to amaze me, I remembered that the man who sat upon this throne—Jafet—relied on city rabble to strike terror into the hearts of his enemies. He had abused the kingship—and he was my quarry, my prey, just inches from me now. But I was without my sword.

"Lorkdan," said Jafet in the tongue of the Zarubes, though his accent was barely understandable. "Lorkdan of Berry Thicket…"

"I speak the tongue of Ardogne," I said.

"Your Majesty! Your Majesty!" Jafet corrected me.

And as soon as he said those words, his servants had swarmed me and whips were lashing me, cutting into my skin. My eyes were watering in pain. At last, I fell to my knees, overcome and wincing, almost sobbing—a shell of what I had been.

"I speak the tongue of Ardogne, Your Majesty," I said, and I said those last two words in bitterness.

"Very well," Jafet replied in his own language. "Lorkdan… of Berry Thicket. You overthrew the Count of Valle."

My name was known everywhere it seemed. It had reached these stately halls—it had reached the ears of this villain, this usurper. I tried the cloth binds, thinking I'd charge him and strangle him with my bare hands, but the binds were tight, on my wrists and on my legs. They were immovable.

"You killed seven of my men, Lorkdan," Jafet said. "That is what it seems you do best—you kill.

"My brother believes he is the rightful king. But the armies lost confidence in him; they turned against him. They set me on the throne.

"But still the common people love him… the tribesmen adore him. And he escaped me before I could kill him—before I could kill him, like you, Lorkdan, have killed so many."

He raised his left hand. From the shadows men in cloaks were approaching. In one of their hands was a bowl.

"Lorkdan, mercenary, who overthrew the Count of Valle," Jafet said. "I would ask of you something but I know what is in your heart—you tried to overthrow me.

"My brother is hiding away in the island regions. If I send an army, he will catch wind of it and flee. But a masterful warrior can overcome his small bodyguard."

"No!" I began to say. "No!" And I feared that bowl—though I did not know why. My fear was like a half-remembered dream.

I struggled anew against my binds, harder than before, intending to leap up and strike Jafet down, with my fist—with anything in arm's reach. I would overthrow him. I would!

But a bowl was pressed against my lips; two hands restrained my head, two more opened my jaw. The bowl was tilted, and liquid entered my mouth, liquid I felt I had tasted before, syrupy—bitter yet sweet.

~

The face before me was wreathed in light; it appeared he

was sitting on a throne. He stood up and raised his hands, one of which held a gleaming scepter. And I knew whatever he said was the truth; I knew whatever he commanded, I would have to do.

"Go," he said, "to the isles that are called Numinous. Hunt down the rebel Diego. Bring back to King Jafet his head."

That was what I would do; it was my task in life.

Part Five

Looking back, I now know what Jafet did to me. I am ashamed, but few can resist such devilry.

—Lorkdan, "Records from Evre Prison"

Chapter Eighteen: The Hunt

The ship was skimming the waters of the sea. The sky and sea alike were cerulean, the color of a brilliant sapphire. The air was warm but getting colder; it seemed like the elements were returning to normal, that the trick of nature that allowed a desert land to form so far north was waning here.

And my mind was focused. These sailors were taking me to one of the islands called Numinous. And I would undertake the mission that now burned in my heart… to kill the false king Diego, and bring his head to the true king Jafet.

Somewhere, on these scattered islands, he and other traitors were hiding. I with my sword would find him; I with my sword would kill him.

Late in the afternoon, the shores of an island appeared, a beach of white sand covered in pines—in the distance tall hills on the verge of being mountains. "Is this where he is?" I said.

And one of the sailors said to me, "I do not know. That is *your* task, Lorkdan of Berry Thicket. You must find him, and bring us back his head."

I would do it. To Diego, I'd be vengeance embodied. His rebellion and treason would cease.

From the ship, lingering out to sea, I left in a boat, and paddled to the shore. My future, and my task, was ahead of me.

~

From the moment I reached the beach, I knew I was in a place of deep wilderness, where few had ever trod before. The birdsong was loud, but I knew a man such as I would not last here long exposed. I was a man of war, not of nature. I was a fighter, not a woodsman. I did not know how to hunt or how to forage for food. I did not know which mushrooms would delight the senses and give strength to my bones and which mushrooms would kill me. All I had was my sword, and my coin purse which would do little. Could I pay one of these pines to offer me directions? Could I offer one of these birds a *denier* in exchange for giving itself as meat?

I was not a woodsman, not acquainted with the wilderness. I did not so much as know how to start a fire without flint and tinder. And I had no flint and tinder, nor did I have road-bread or salt pork, the traveler's companion. All I had was my clothing, my sword, and a burning fire in my heart—the desire above all else to track Diego down, to bring him low, to bring his head back to Asina Aurea for all the people to see. That was my task—and I would do it.

I eyed the woods.

Would I, no woodsman, be able to gain a living there? I doubted it.

Somewhere on this isle was Diego — or so Jafet's men thought.

I ventured forth, toward the trees.

~

The boughs of the pines were moist with recent rain. The air had a scent of wildflowers, and on the ground was dew. Pine needles, red, formed a carpet of sorts on the forest floor. And I was in a kind of place I had not seen much, unspoiled wilderness where there were no farms or houses or buildings or shops. It was a place I was ill equipped to survive, but one where a man such as Diego could easily hide. Somewhere on this isle, he was hiding. And my desire to bring him low was like a burning fire in my heart. But I could not remember what had placed that desire within me. I remembered a light wreathed figure. And I remembered another light wreathed figure, too.

And I said "Briar Rose." Why had I said *briar rose?*

But when I said it, the winds seemed to pick up, and the pines swayed in its wake. The darkness of the forest was deep. I would not be able to catch game, but there was plentiful water.

I ventured deeper into the woods.

~

In clearings where the sun's light shone, brilliant green moss clung to rocks and logs. Slugs and snails were in abundance, even bright yellow slugs the color of lemons. The air was moist but it was cool. I wondered if those slithering creatures would be good to eat. I had seen people in the Royal City eat more questionable things — the bizarre things they ate, prepared in many ways, were a point of pride to them.

But I could not imagine myself eating a slimy snail, or a slug covered in ichor. I was not that hungry, and I prayed I'd never be.

The isle was well-watered, and throughout the forests were many streams and ponds, and small watering holes. The mountains I traversed, low mountains like those in the Barrens but which were covered in trees and brilliant greenery.

Light showers began to fall in the afternoon, and I was isolated, alone, in the deep woods.

But through bushes, past two hawthorn trees, I made out something that distinguished itself — dirt.

If a path it was little better than a deer path, but man or animal had made use of it. This isle was inhabited, by man or perhaps by deer, and I vowed I would follow this makeshift road. The Via tribe had left me with some coin. Perhaps, there was some cotter or farmer in the middle of these woods, someone who wouldn't balk at a *sou* or *denier*, who had use for gold or silver and would take my money in exchange for food.

Bushes and the branches of trees brushed against me as I hurried along the meager path, underneath a canopy or a sky that was alternately sunny or cloudy. The wind was whipping up a storm, and rain was beginning to spray me.

The path was taking me into the mountains, and if it was a road, it was the crudest of roads. I surmised hunters lived here, eking out a living — bandits perhaps, escaping the law.

As it ascended, the air grew chillier and chillier, and the wind was cutting into my neck. I had no doubt there were bears on this island — cougars perhaps, and mountain lions, too. It was halfway between Ardogne's dry climate and the rainy forests of the west, for in addition to pines there were those thorny green plants, flowering rosebushes, and dwarf palms.

At one point, late in the day, I was growing haggard, panting, sweating, when I reached a vista and saw the gleaming sea below. I could see the white sand beach where I had embarked on this journey, and now it seemed impossibly far, that I had made a great voyage.

And I did not know if I was headed to a destination, or only to starvation and imminent death.

I had no food, and few supplies, and no way of catching animals, nor knowledge of how to hunt. All I had was my sword — the tool of my trade, a trade I had plied since I was a young man, which would not help me in the wilderness, or so I thought.

Up I traveled, and the path's ascent was sharp. Amid greenery and moss and lichen, I was quickly approaching the mountain's summit. The path, I had determined, was not a deer path, for along it, I had seen signs of littering, potsherds and discarded apple cores, bits of bread, and the clear indent of boots in the mud.

The sun began to dip below the sea, and the path's ascent grew even sharper, until I — a warrior and athlete — was wondering if I had the energy to go on, or if I should stop here, find some spot in the middle of the woods to sleep, underneath a pine or a hawthorn tree. Soon it would be night — and where would I lay my head? My stomach growled; I was getting terribly hungry. But I began to smell something on the wind — something, a scent I had smelled before, harsh, pungent, one I recognized. Was it incense?

I redoubled my movements, hurrying and not walking, despite the cramps that had developed in my side, despite the sweat pouring from my skin and the tenderness in my calves. There was hope — hope of something more than moss and lichen, hope of something more than pines and hawthorns and dwarf palms.

I was drawing near to something and I did not know what.

~

The moon was rising, the skies were dark, and the stars were like beacons against a black canvas. The trees became sparser until they had vanished completely. And my hurried walk had morphed into a run. In a place laden with the scent of wildflowers, I saw it: a stone building on the mountain's summit.

The walls were high, of stone, and in the center of the building was a tower. Before it was an iron fence and a great gate, and posted outside were two guards, but they were sleeping.

In the cool of the night air, I stood, obscured by the darkness—they had not noticed me, nor could they. They were slumped in their seats, eyes closed, not expecting visitors, and why would they?

I tried, looking upon the structure, to guess its intent. It was on the height of this mountain, on one of the islands that are called Numinous. I supposed there was only one way to find out.

~

I, Lorkdan, am a mercenary, but I do not spill blood if it is not required. In fights in taverns, I always tried to avoid beating someone to the point of death, not only for fear of the law, but because it was Balzor's, and the gods, to determine when a life would be snuffed out. Blood I did not delight in; coin was what I desired.

That was the man I had been. But standing there, in the night darkness, I recalled I had been given a task—to kill Diego and those who protected him. Why had I? A light-wreathed figure.

"Briar Rose," I said under my breath. Why had I said *briar rose?*

A guard jerked awake; he heaved his spear into his hands and began to bark in a dialect of the language of Ardogne which I could scarcely understand.

I drew back and heard the growl of a dog—something that had always caused me to shrivel in fear. I could see the dog's eyes, dark yet bright, gleaming, and those eyes reminded me of something, a woman's voice, a request that I had forgotten.

"What are you doing?" one of the guards shouted. "Who are you?"

I drew back from the snarling dog. "I am Lorkdan. I have come…. I have come…"

Deceit was not my strength. In the moonlight, I saw reliefs of bulls on the walls. Was this a shrine to Toro?

"I have come to make an offering," I said.

I lifted up my coinpurse, heard its contents jingle.

The guard grabbed the dog by its collar, said something to it, and it calmed down.

"An offering, you say," the guard said. "The Astral Observatory needs no money."

An observatory for the stars, set high on this mountain. I wondered what discoveries they had made, and what they had learned. It was a fitting place to observe, so dark, in the middle of the mountains, with no light to pollute the starlight.

"I think you had best get going," said the guard.

I backed down at the sight of the dog, at the sight of the spears which both guards wielded.

"I am terribly hungry," I said. "I have no shelter."

The guard's eyes twinkled in the night darkness. "Are you alone, 'Lorkdan?'"

Apparently, some were not aware of my exploits. There were places where the legend of Lorkdan of Berry Thicket had not spread, and I was glad of it.

"I am alone," I said.

"And what are you doing on Cavero Isle?"

~

I was let through the doors of the observatory, and there before me was a room of flagstone, a wooden table in its center, on it a bowl.

And the master of the observatory, having been woken, walked up to me. "I think you have not been truthful, 'Lorkdan.' You did not wash up here on these shores like Amara on the half-shell. There is a reason you had come.

"We in the observatory are charged with taking care of travelers and guarding the way. But before we give you a little food, you must tell me why you have come here."

I looked into the man's dark eyes, saw his purple robe edged in green. On his head was a nightcap; he was dressed for sleep.

And I, Lorkdan, was not one to deceive. I did not have a glib tongue. "Jafet sent me," I told him.

"Jafet," said the master of the observatory, and a scowl was writ on his features. "The false king. He reigns in the City on his throne of lies, but his power is not here on the isles called Numinous, which our ancestors have considered sacred since unremembered time.

"No; we of the isles honor the true king, Diego."

Diego—Jafet's brother. The passion with which I was going about this mission befuddled me. I thought of a light-wreathed figure, words spoken—words I had considered a message of the gods.

Diego—I had to kill him. It was my goal in life.

The memories of before were like a cloudy glass.

"Briar Rose," I said.

Why had I said *briar rose*?

"Lorkdan," said the master of the observatory, "I think there is something wrong with you. I fear I know what it is.

"You are a foreigner. A *grieo*. Do you remember coming to this land?"

Of course I did—of course I remembered. The Royal City… crossing the border past a Narrow Stream. But all was cloudy, all inscrutable.

"Diego," I said to the master of the observatory. "You must tell me where he is."

"Long live Diego, King of Ardogne, now and in the future." The master of the observatory was glaring at me. "Arrest him! Bind him!"

The guards struck with their spears; the dog was set loose, but in an eye's blink my sword was in my hands, and in the span of moments the injured dog had fled, and the two guards were slashed and bleeding, dying on the floor.

To his credit, the master of the observatory did not turn and flee, screaming into the night. No, he stood there and without sword or dagger he faced me bravely.

"I know what ails you, Lorkdan," he said. "A poison of the mind. Your actions are not your own!"

"Where is Diego?" I said to him. And the way he shrunk back and seemed to shrivel told me that he knew.

"You are not yourself," he said. "You have been poisoned."

He knew where my quarry was—he knew where Diego had been hiding. He turned and gave chase; I followed him through a hallway, up a stone staircase, past candles on sconces and lanterns in alcoves, upwards, upwards, upwards, and though I could have easily overtaken him, I wanted his fear to build. I wanted the fear to mold into panic—and then I could force the truth from his lips.

Like a lurking phantom, I followed him, and my shadow greeted me on the other side of the wall, flickering and bending and twisting as I followed the observatory-keeper.

At last we reached the top of the tower, where there was a spyglass. He had grabbed a torch—and in the darkness I saw a bundle of logs. A signal fire—he was trying to light a signal fire! The people of the Numinous Isles, who remained loyal to Diego, were protecting their king.

I tackled the master of the observatory to the ground. The torch slipped from his hands, and slid just inches from the oil-soaked wood. I dropped my sword, pinned him to the ground, and said to him, "Where is he? Tell me."

His face had gone a shade of white. His fingers were trembling.

I grabbed the torch, which was just within arm's reach. I held its burning fire up to the observatory-keeper's face, just inches from it.

"Where is he? Tell me!" I said.

The flame was singeing his skin, enough for pain, but not for lasting damage.

"Where is he? Tell me!"

But the night was drifting on, the stars in the sky riding by in their royal procession.

"Where is he? Tell me!" And as I stood there, torch in hand, I realized the body beneath me was not moving, that my knee had blocked his throat.

He was dead; he was no use to me now.

What a monster I'd become.

Chapter Nineteen: Prey

In the observatory kitchen, I found food—bread well-preserved, meat that was dried, and dried fruits, too. There was wine, but I wouldn't have any. I felt dirty—filthy—after what I had done. I had taken a life and the taking of that life hadn't been warranted. I had killed a man, and for what? I began to eat, to nibble at the bread though I felt I wasn't hungry anymore.

What had I done? A monstrous act… one that even Balzor god of the underworld would not approve of. Or would he?

It was late, and I was growing tired. On a divan I sat down and slumped over. My eyelids felt heavy, so very heavy.

~

I woke to a loud pounding on the door. In the confusion of sleep, I did not know where I was, maybe in The Belled Dancer, or at my mother's house in Berry Thicket.

Then I saw the bodies of the guards on the floor, the blood smeared on the rough flagstone. I was in an observatory in the Numinous Isles—that's where I was.

And someone was knocking on the door.

Someone—knocking on the door.

As quickly as I could, I hauled the distended bodies into the kitchen, though there was blood still to be seen.

I did not know whether to answer the door, but I had a feeling… another inexplicable feeling.

To the door I hurried, and opened it just slightly.

A man was standing there, dusky, a man of Ardogne, in a robe of red, and a scimitar at his side.

Suspicion appeared in his eyes, and he was gawking at me

questioningly.

"Who are you?" he said.

"The observatory-keeper." I was poor at dreaming up deceptions, but good at bluffing.

"The observatory-keeper," the man replied. "Dario?"

"That's I," I said.

"A *grieo*," he said.

"Yes," I answered him. "When I came to Ardogne I changed my name. Didn't Diego tell you?"

A gambit, a guess… that this man knew of Diego, that he knew where he was hiding.

"No, he did not," the man said. The suspicion waned in his eyes. "We saw a torch on the observatory tower… we wanted to ensure we weren't compromised."

"No one's come," I told him.

The suspicion returned anew. And he drew back just slightly.

"Will you let me have a look?" the man said.

"Certainly," I said.

And the door opened, and the man entered. When he looked in shock at the blood, I beat him over the head with the pommel of my sword. Two strokes, and he was dead.

I felt filthier than ever before, dirty—but if I let him live, he would have told Diego, and my quarry would escape.

~

I ventured upwards, to the roof of the observatory, and in the sun's light I could see much of the island, white sand beaches and forests, and small cays off the shore. The day had significantly warmed.

Somewhere on this island was Diego—but to my left I saw

motion, two men sprinting down the mountain path. I had not seen them; they had seen me. Perhaps, they had heard anguished cries coming from the observatory, and now they intended to let their king know.

I scrambled down the stairs of the observatory, out the door. With my sword in hand, I took off after them in a sprint. It would be them or me—I, the hunter, or them, my prey. One of us was faster and swifter, and one of us would be overcome.

~

My side was aching, my breath harsh in my lungs, sweat covering my body, and my tunic drenched, when I reached a high hill, and saw the two men below me. They were running towards the shore; they were running towards a cay.

And I stopped a moment to catch my breath, to restore my energy.

Under the sunlight, in the blue sky, I saw it… a forested cay, out to shore, which those men were swimming towards.

And I was certain beyond certainty that that was where Diego was hiding… behind those trees, he was there.

I let the swimmers go; I watched as they entered the cay, and ran into the woods. Then I made my move.

~

Now drenched in saltwater and not sweat, my boots touched the white sand of the cay. I removed my sword from its sling, and held it in both hands. And into the trees I ran, the towering pines and dwarf palms, as a fair wind gusted, and I was brought quickly to my destination.

A dozen soldiers guarded Diego's camp, men in armor with steel swords and shields, and they ran at me at once. They had not known the legend of Lorkdan of Berry Thicket; they had not known what I was capable of.

A man went down, bleeding; I slashed again and pierced another through the heart. Another strike, another parry, and three were dead at my feet, then four.

A storm of steel, and my arm was cut. A storm of steel, and I was slashed across the face—another scar soon would form. A storm of steel, and the soldiers had either died, or were scattered. Their bodies lay at my feet.

Diego was now at my mercy.

But I could not remember why I was doing this. I didn't understand my great desire.

But that desire propelled me forward, through the forest, past scattered bodies, to a place where there was a wooden fence— a wooden fence, and beyond it, splendor.

There was a seat of wood in the clearing, a seat edged in gold. The sunlight shining through the trees was like a celestial radiance, coming down from heaven above. And a man sat on that seat, a man in a purple robe—purple, which only kings wear. He was handsome, darkly-featured, with black hair and bright eyes.

The richest clothing was available to him, the richest clothing—and gold and silver rings. But beside him was someone more remarkable, more remarkable not for the things she possessed but for the beauty that had been given to her by the gods.

She was slight and petite, and her hair was red, and her eyes were a sky blue. She wore a green gown, and like King Diego she showed no sign of fear of me. Instead, she was looking at me questioningly—looking through me and not at me.

I passed through the wooden gate. The false king was now defenseless. But he did not turn to run. He stared at me in the eye and said, "Who are you?"

"Lorkdan," I said, "the underworld's champion."

"What an epithet," said King Diego. "I hope it is not deserved."

And I saw that there were others in this camp, men and women alike, and a few children. They were all looking at me, anticipating something terrible, the bloodshed I had vowed to execute.

Yet I looked into Diego's eyes, and saw that they were bright. Fair-faced was he, handsome, and though he was older than his brother, he did not appear quite so wizened. He had not been so hardened by scheming and by hatred. His youth was not in body but in soul.

I approached him, sword in hand, knowing what deed I had to do, knowing that this is what had been asked of me.

"Will you kill me, Lorkdan?" Diego said.

"I will," I replied. My sword was dripping blood.

"And why will you kill me?" Diego said. "Why? Think!"

It was an absurd situation—the quarry asking the hunter why he did what he did. And yet I was not moving, I was not striking. I was looking at Diego, and then also the beautiful woman beside him.

"I…"

Why was I doing this? Why, truly? Had I ever cared about anything but gold or silver? Why was the murder of Diego the thing I desired above all else? Why was I so intent on killing him? It made little sense at all.

"What is the last thing you remember," said Diego, "before you set out to commit regicide?"

Why was I heeding his questions? Why was I hesitating? I supposed it was because they were at my mercy, and I could afford to.

All these people, men, women, and children, were at the mercy of my sword, and the one who wielded it.

What had happened to me when I set out to kill Diego? What was the last thing I remembered?

A bitter taste, harsh like gall. Liquid dripping down my throat.

No—it couldn't be.

And other things, memories half formed… a tribe of people moving about the desert. And there was the memory of that bitter taste then too, thick liquid dripping into my mouth.

"The sap of the *cara* tree changes who imbibes it," Diego said. "Most cannot resist. Some are lucky and immune, but that is not most of us.

"I fear someone has taken you, Lorkdan, the underworld's champion, and turned you into something you never were. You are a mighty warrior, that is clear. Twelve dead by your hand. But you have been twisted. You have been deceived. Do not commit any more bloodshed this day."

Memories were returning, as if through a looking glass… faded, but clearing up. I had been in Jafet's throne room. And my desire at that time had been for something else.

But a bowl was placed to my lips. A harsh taste, bitter, like gall, a thick liquid running down my throat.

"Do you see now?" Diego said. "Do you see now, underworld's champion? As King of Ardogne, I will show you mercy, because your actions were not your own."

Not my own… not my own…

I did not trust his words, or the thoughts he was planting in my mind. But all memory was a foggy glass… a light-wreathed figure… *briar rose*.

Still my heart burned with desire; still I felt it was my mission to kill this man. But I was hesitating; my sword was in my hands, but my hands were trembling.

And I was looking at Diego in a new way. My resolve was weakening.

"Your mind was poisoned, Lorkdan, underworld's champion," Diego said. "What drives you is not your own will, but the words of a deceiver, and the bitterness of *cara* sap.

"Don't you see it? Don't you see it?"

I was not striking him down; I was not lobbing off his head and bringing it back to Jafet. I remembered that my purposes in coming to this foreign land had initially been something else.

I had treated Jafet's words like the words of the gods.

It had not been a light-wreathed figure telling me to kill Diego… it had been Jafet, with the help of *cara* sap.

And I stood there, waiting, wondering just what I would do. And I struggled against the poison that still lingered in my mind.

And the foggy memories began to grow clear… a tall mug of ale. Beautiful girls hopping table to table.

An expedition into the heartland of Zarubain, which had been met with failure.

A mercenary with a lobster like helm… a young would-be king whom I had been told to kill.

And there was something else, a cloudy memory clearing up, a foggy glass becoming clear. And I remembered the woman, and I remembered the name Allórie.

And in the span of a moment, I recalled why I had come here to this land.

She had wanted a rose of gold, a rose with a gold stem and a red blossom. And it had been in the possession of the "King of Ardogne…" once Diego.

"Diego," I said, "I remember now."

Diego smiled, and light touched his eyes. Compared to him, his brother was a wizened monster, aged not by years but by hatred and scheming.

"I came to this foreign land," I said, "to where I don't belong, because I was sent here. There is a woman in the Royal City who said you had taken something from her. A rose forged of gold, with a red blossom. Briar Rose."

"Briar Rose," Diego said, and his smile grew, and the light in his eyes brightened until they were sparkling. "Lorkdan, you and that woman are mistaken.

"I have no such rose, nor would I have use for it. You came here for a false reason. But perhaps, the gods guided you here for a different reason entirely. Perhaps, the true king of Ardogne has need for a *grieo*, one who can speak the tongue of our erstwhile enemy… the kingdom of the north, Zarubain."

~

By the *cara* sap's deception, I had done ill. I had murdered twelve men, bodyguards of Diego whom he had relied on for protection. But the king seemed generous, and willing to forgive, for my actions had not been my own.

Together, we walked along the white sand beach, underneath the blue sky, and I learned of Diego's plans, and what he had intended to do.

In view of a dwarf palm, he announced his plans. "An emissary of King Bretagne is coming here," Diego said. "Perhaps, by the might of Zarubain the true king of Ardogne can be restored to his throne."

Such a thing would be considered treason by the common. But I supposed, if the rightful king was restored, it would be worth it. The Red Guards would no longer terrorize Asina Aurea; tavernkeepers and priests would be left in peace.

"An emissary is coming, you say," I told Diego.

And more memories were returning, memories I rather didn't like, of what I had done.

I had entered the temple that was near Asina Aurea… men had been dead by my hand, even the man who played Toro.

Many lives taken… but my task here was not finished.

"An emissary coming," I said.

"A man close to the king," Diego said. "Elisette is a *grieo*, like you, but she has lived so long in Asina Aurea, with me, that her speech has eroded. And I believe they would respect more a man of war like yourself."

I remembered I had been conscripted into the king's service.

Elisette, presumably, was the beautiful red-haired woman who had been standing next to him.

"He is coming at break of dawn," said Diego, "to hear our request. Perhaps, to act on it.

"Lorkdan, you have gravely injured me. A dozen men, my finest, dead… but I can see now your talent with the sword is great. You wield it like a masterful artist wields his brush, like a scribe wields his quill.

"A pity my brother poisoned your mind."

"Others poisoned me as well." Only one request had been pure, without deception. Only one mission I had gone about with my own free will.

That mission had been from the woman Allórie, dark haired, dark eyed. I had come here for the Briar Rose, and though Diego denied he had it, it was still on my mind.

~

That night, at camp, eating road-bread and salt pork, and helping ourselves to wine, I scanned every man and woman for a rose of gold. And when I walked from table to table, I looked under them, and about them. But I could see no rose of gold, with a red blossom.

Still, I would not give up. Only the woman Allórie's quest had been pure, and I would not forget it.

Chapter Twenty: The Plot

The dawn brought clouds, and a red sun rising over the sea. It brought a rose-colored sky, and something else it brought as well. Ships had appeared, warships with towering sails.

As I stood there, witnessing the approaching armada, more foggy memories became unclouded. I had stopped at an inn, and a tavern girl had told me the king of Zarubain "wished to speak to me." And I remembered I had stayed my hand… I had not killed the one the king of Zarubain demanded.

Yet I could do nothing, now. I had agreed to be King Diego's translator. If the King of Zarubain would punish me, I would have to face it.

From one of the larger ships, a smaller craft was rowing in, a man, a *grieo* like me, in a black cap and a dark blue cloak. Behind him were knights in full armor, with swords at their sides, four in number.

And on the ships in the distance I could see sailors, but in addition to those were men-at-arms and peasant soldiers, knights with ornately decorated shields and horses beside. An army had come with this emissary; it seemed that King Bretagne had already decided upon King Diego's request.

Diego would wage war against his nation, what some might call an act of treason… and for King Bretagne to expend his men this way, there was surely a cost. Diego would be a puppet on a string.

The boat landed and the emissary stepped out; he bowed just slightly, an act of reverence. He was pallid, and his hair was a lush brown. His eyes sparkled blue.

"King," the emissary said in his own tongue, "the true King of Ardogne."

And I repeated those words to Diego in his own language.

As the conversation wore on, from King Bretagne's announcement of help to the discussion of logistics, the seriousness of what Diego was doing was seeming to weigh on him. The young light in his eyes just seemed to wane.

What would the people of Asina Aurea think, the Red Guards who terrorized the streets or even the devout mobs who opposed them? What would the people of Ardogne in general think, even the tribesmen, if Diego came back at the front of a foreign army—and not just any foreign army, but *grieos*, Zarubain, their longtime enemy?

I supposed, in the coming days, and weeks, I would find out.

"We go at once," said the emissary, whose name I learned was Lucenne. "Thank you, Diego, true king of Ardogne... and thank you, Lorkdan, the underworld's champion..."

Lucenne, the emissary, seemed to grin at the sight of me. He, and the one who had sent him, were not done with me, yet.

~

On three dozen warships, an army of some five thousand men-at-arms and two hundred knights, together with catapults and battering rams, set sail for Asina Aurea, underneath a blue sky and a bright sun. I, Lorkdan, the underworld's champion, counted down the hours on the flagship, with King Diego beside me. I had been let into his private circle, though I had done injury to him in my poisoned state.

Elisette was with us, and beautiful she was. She was ready for the day of battle, not in armor, but in a silken gown colored gold.

Part Six

The ships sailed swiftly, and when they reached the City of Asina Aurea, the soldiers were deployed. For seven days and seven nights, there was fire and bloodshed... desperation.

The gate was broken by dawn of the eighth day, and by noon the false king Jafet was hanging from a tree.

—Lorkdan, "Records from Evre Prison"

Chapter Twenty-One: Restoration

When Diego entered Castle Ambra, he seemed quiet, even chastened. And when he sat on the throne, before the dazzling breadth and splendor of the throne room, I thought I saw regret in his eyes. I was to protect him, I, Lorkdan, the underworld's champion. I was a *grieo*, like those he used to conquer the city and restore himself to the throne.

Elisette seemed uncomfortable at the sight of Zarube soldiers and men-at-arms walking about the splendor of Castle Ambra's marble halls.

But I, Lorkdan, remembered why I had first come.

"Briar Rose," I said, standing guard over King Diego, so quiet he couldn't hear.

Why did I seek after the Briar Rose? It was for the woman Allórie, that's why, who had offered to me her home, and her drink. No light-wreathed figure had told me to do this, nor was I motivated by gold or silver reward. Only the memory of her charity drove me on… and when Diego retired to bed in his occupied palace, I vowed to search.

Perhaps, Diego did not know he was in possession of the Briar Rose. Perhaps, somewhere in the Castle Ambra, it was hidden and forgotten.

~

As I walked the marble halls, beside colonnades of pointed arches and statues of Toro and of kings, castle servants would glare at me as they spoke among themselves. Jafet was dead; he had been hanged. But how long before the people rose up, angry people under occupation, under the thumb of a foreign power?

If I, a mere bodyguard, was glared at, what enmity did they have for the *grieo* soldiers now walking freely about the Castle Ambra? How long before they served Diego a death cap, or knifed him in his bed?

The situation was unsustainable, but I tried to put those thoughts aside, tried to forget them, as I wandered from library to gaming hall to forgotten room, searching for any sign of the Briar Rose, a rose of gold with a red bloom.

It was late, and I was ready to give up, when I passed through the door and felt the cool night air kiss me. Above head, the stars were gleaming, and the moon was white and full. In the garden were rose bushes and saffron crocus, chamomile and lemon balm and mint bushes, together with trees on which bright yellow fruit grew, which I had not known of.

In the far corner were scattered dark figures, and the sound of a lute rising above the wind.

I walked up to one of the fruiting trees, and plucked one of the fruits from its branches. I tore apart its peel, and bit in… I puckered, and my eyes watered. It was so sour, it did not seem good to eat—but many such trees were in the castle garden.

From the dark shadows, a silhouette was approaching—I was not alone.

Her beauty stole my breath, her long red hair still vibrant in color in the dimness of the night. "Lorkdan," she said to me, "how do you like the drupe pear?"

"Well, I suppose I must admit, I don't like it too much," I said, "and I can't imagine why it would be growing in the garden."

She smiled—her name was Elisette, I recalled. "It is not good for eating," she said, "not in the manner you're eating it. When squeezed and chilled, and when water and lumps of sugar are added to it, it makes a fine summer drink."

"It is almost summer," I stated as a fact, but it amazed me I'd spent so much time here, in this foreign land. And I wondered what the Royal City was facing now.

More memories were returning… a famine… hungry bodies, gaunt and pale. People malnourished. And war-drums—but the Empire seemed a more distant threat now.

Elisette smiled. "Are you from the Royal City?" she said to me.

"I am from elsewhere," I told her. "A land far away… I came west to the serve in Zarubain's armies… and flights of fancy and strange feelings led me to this place.

"I was sent to find the Briar Rose…"

"The Briar Rose," Elisette uttered. "I think you will find it, if you seek after it with all your heart."

What was she saying? Yet she had begun to smile, and that smile was growing.

"Do you know where I can find the Briar Rose?" I said.

"I think I do," she said.

The sound of the lute was growing louder; the wind, cold, was kissing my cheek.

My stomach was full, and I lacked nothing. A feather bed was waiting for me, perfumed with aloes, clean and comfortable on this early summer night.

"Will you go with me on a horseback ride," said Elisette, "tomorrow, at dawn?"

"I prefer donkeys," I said, "but yes."

I had been a terrible master. Lily was capable, and strong, and she rarely strayed from me, and where I would leave her she would remain.

But I had not looked after her.

In the morning I found her, still in the grassland outside the city. Elisette had joined me on a horse, a shapely brown horse. And romance seemed to be blossoming, but Elisette would not be easily won. I did not consider her a prize, though—I would treat her with respect.

On Lily I followed Elisette, but her horse was much swifter than a donkey.

I followed her, coaxing Lily, up a hill, around the ring of the mountainous ground. At last, on a high hill, we stopped, and I saw then that Elisette had brought a basket of bread and sliced meats.

"A good vantage point," said Elisette, "of the City… and Diego's tragic victory."

"Why is it tragic?" I said.

"When I was young," said Elisette, "or younger… King Diego was visiting the Royal City. I caught his eye and he caught mine. I left all I knew, to be his concubine, maybe one day wife— but we were never wed. I came to a troubled land… the Red Guards were in their infancy then, and he and Jafet were even on speaking terms.

"Look at this, Lorkdan… this city under occupation. It is not the Ardogne I came to in my youth. Now it is something else… a tragic victory indeed. And the world I left has come here… to this place of sunny skies and warmth. The world I left… knights and men-at-arms and soldiers.

"Diego resorted to this… and I cannot look at him the same. I don't see him as I used to."

The way she told the story, it did seem a tragedy… a naïve and beautiful girl, wooed by a foreign king, and brought to a land where trouble was brewing, pent-up unrest waiting to burst free. Diego had been driven from the throne, the Red Guards had won; but now, his brother had lost, and was hanging from a tree.

"A foreign army occupying the city," said Elisette, "it will drive anyone with a love of country into the hands of the Red Guards.

"But what other choice did my love have? He could have abandoned Ardogne, but if he fled he would not be safe anywhere. Jafet's greatest desire was for his brother's death."

"He made the right choice," I said. "For him, and for Ardogne."

"He has not put a salve on Ardogne's wounds," Elisette said. "He has stirred the fire.

"The people hate *grieos* and *grieas* like you or me."

"Do not worry," I said. "Do not worry… it does no good. If chaos comes, make the best of it."

But it was easy for me to say.

"Let's eat," said Elisette.

"Will you tell me where the Briar Rose is?" I said.

"You are getting closer," she replied. "It is almost in your hands."

What a strange thing for Elisette to say.

But we ate, and the bread was crispy and filling, the slices of meat perfectly seasoned. And I caught Elisette looking at me in a way that wasn't proper for Diego's concubine.

But she had said I was getting close to the Briar Rose… it was "almost in my hands."

~

We returned to the castle, and I put Lily up in the castle stable, for I didn't trust any stable in Asina Aurea. The common folk detested people like me.

The foggy memories cleared… and I recalled one woman of Ardogne who had loved *grieos*, a woman who ran a tavern. We had made love.

I had returned to a storm; as I wandered the halls, Diego's loyalists were moving about shiftily, with uncertain expressions on their faces, gazing at the foreigners who occupied Castle Ambra in trepidation. Others, whose loyalties I did not know, most especially the kitchen scullions and the lowest ranking workers, were glaring at me and others like me as I moved about. I couldn't imagine what the common people of Ardogne were saying in the privacy of their homes, in taverns like The Crimson Cup where—I remembered— the woman like Yacinda had worked.

And I wondered what the Red Guards were plotting, the gangs who had terrorized Asina Aurea's streets, and put Diego's brother on the throne. But Diego's brother, Jafet, was dead, hanging and putrefied from a tree, for all to see.

I did not know if the number of troops that King Bretagne had sent were adequate to squash the inevitable rebellion. But as the day wore on, I couldn't help but think that Elisette desired to depart the country altogether, and as she moved about the castle, there seemed to be worry writ on her features.

The tension in Castle Ambra was palpable. The city was surely ready to break into a riot—a well-oiled log which would burst alight at the slightest spark.

Elisette wished to flee, I was sure—but I would not leave without the Briar Rose. That, after all, was the reason most pure, the cause for me coming here—not the tribesmen, not Jafet, not Diego. Elisette had said "it was almost in my hands"—what had she meant?

Night set, and I left Diego's side; I departed the throne room. I returned to my private quarters on the highest level of Castle Ambra. I thought I'd sharpen my sword.

~

With a stone I sharpened it, from the vantage point of my high balcony. The night sky was dark, but the lights of the city were bright. Asina Aurea did not sleep, like its sister to the north, the Royal City.

I could see the harbor, a lighthouse—and in the sparkling moonlit waters were far fewer ships than when I'd first arrived. Much of the city had been pulverized by the siege, entire neighborhoods laid waste, and none were attempting to rebuild.

What was being said now, under cover of dark? What outrages were being discussed in private homes, in the lights of taverns? When would a stray spark fall, and the city erupt?

But those in Asina Aurea were not well armed. Jafet's men had cut down the roving mob… now, though, Jafet's men were dead.

Such destruction, such pain. Ardogne now seemed home to a powerless people… but often the gods would hear anguished cries. Often, they would answer the prayers of the desperate.

Asina Aurea was quiet, under the boot of Zarube knights, with swords to their necks. Yet I had a feeling I couldn't shake, of an impending storm, anger palpable in the night air—the anger of a people not yet defeated. Did Diego think even his former supporters would accept his foreign-backed rule—and not just any foreigners, but *grieos* like Elisette or I?

My sword now gleamed in the moonlight, sharp, keen. I prayed I'd not use it any time soon, especially not against the common people of Asina Aurea, who had suffered all too many indignities already.

The moon was white and shining. The stars were gleaming. And I could see in the sky that the constellation of the Eagle was rising.

Chapter Twenty-Two: Taken

As bodyguard I followed Diego to his meetings, as he tried to wrangle control of a nation that had been forever changed, not the nation he had ruled before his brother seized control. He ordered the cessation of the wars on the tribesmen, that they be allowed to graze their cattle in peace—that their meadowlands not be turned into farms.

It was the afternoon, and hot, when the Zarube emissary Lucenne approached. We were in a room called the Chamber of Stars, and the ceiling was brightly painted in stars of gold leaf.

"King Diego," said Lucenne, "our ally. My liege Bretagne is glad to have restored the rightful King of Ardogne to his throne.

"But we must make a request from you."

Here it was—and I was here to witness it. In the game of kings and princes, of nations and dominions, nothing was ever free, nothing was charitably given. All help had a cost. And Bretagne had helped Diego immeasurably.

Diego seemed to shrink just slightly. Over the days and hours, he seemed to realize what he had done, what situation he had found himself in.

"Our people are starving," said Lucenne, "the wheat crop failed… but I know that in this land there is a surplus. Granaries… stores from many years. You can afford to share it with us."

For the first time, there was a hint of indignation in Diego's eyes, though he'd suffered many indignities quietly and practically submitted to a foreign king. This time, when he spoke, there was a harshness to his tone: "We were wise… we stored those grains over countless months. Our crop failed too, but we were able to manage. You will not rob my people… they are still my people."

Lucenne's blue eyes sparkled; a dark grin appeared on his

face. "Will we depose you then, Diego?"

And I followed him under guard, as the day wore on. The agreement was made; grain was unloaded from the granaries. Ships departed at dusk.

Diego had won the throne; but what a terrible victory it was.

I pitied him, yes—I pitied a king.

~

In the castle garden, I took a drupe pear from the tree, and though they weren't considered fit for eating raw, I had taken a liking to eating them just as they were.

As I peeled it and bit into the pungent fruit, I could see I was not alone. A few courtiers were gathered, singing songs in the darkness, and one was playing a lute.

My eyes watered at the sour taste. Again, like the night before, a shadow appeared, one which became visible in the moonlight. Elisette was wearing a long gown of gold, and her red hair was tied up in a caul.

"Do you often come to the garden?" I said.

"Only when you are here, Lorkdan," she said.

She smiled, and her eyes sparkled. Her lips were red, though not as fiery red as her hair.

"Where is the Briar Rose?" I said to her.

And I wondered if she did not know, if she was only teasing me, if she only was toying with me, tormenting me.

"You are so close," she said.

And she drew near me, and kissed me on the lips.

"Lorkdan," she said, "underworld's champion. I am sorry for being so forward."

"It's quite all right. I only wonder what Diego would think."

"He would not mind," said Elisette. "We have not made love in years. I think I no longer please him, now that I am getting older… and he has a supply of beautiful young women always eager for his attention. Now, my role is his trusted advisor. I tell him when he is wrong. I stop him from making a mistake."

"And do you think he is making a mistake, now?"

"A grave error," she replied, "one he knows deep down. If the people are angry that a foreign army backed his rule, imagine how they'll feel when they learn the granaries are emptied.

"I warned him not to accept Bretagne's help. Perhaps, he had no choice. Perhaps, he was backed into a corner."

"And here we are," I said.

"And here we are, Lorkdan, underworld's champion. I fear as advisor I have not served him well. What has been set in motion cannot be stopped.

"The 'god' Toro dead… foreign troops in Castle Ambra. The Red Guards strengthened and the people driven into their arms."

I had played a part in one of those tragedies.

"And what do you think he should do, now?" I said.

"It is too late," Elisette said, and I saw that her smile was not happy, but sad. "He is trapped. Bretagne has no love for him… his time is nearly up. At someone's hand he will be dead."

"And what will you do?" I said.

"I will stand beside him," replied Elisette, "to the death. His fate and my fate will be the same."

"Your fates are not bound," I said. "You are not pledged together. He did not marry you. Don't die for him."

The smile vanished, and she began to glare. "Lorkdan, you burst into our private life, crazed by *cara* sap, kill twelve of Diego's men… he forgives you knowing you were poisoned, and now you try to turn me against him."

"Not against him," I said. "Just telling you, dying for him is not your duty."

"Don't tell me what my duty is," she said.

And she stormed off. That kiss, it seemed, would never turn into something more.

The stars were shining; the Eagle was even more prominent.

I departed the courtyard and walked off, toward my private room.

~

On the balcony I watched, a city under occupation. And now, unlike before, I saw dark shadows moving about the streets.

I remembered the tavern called The Crimson Cup, I remembered Yacinda. And I wondered how she would manage, how she would navigate the coming storm, if she had turned from her love of Diego and now despised him, if now she wished that Jafet had remained on the throne. I wondered, north of here, if the tribesmen would reject Diego's help.

I wondered what was in store.

And the stars that comprised the Eagle constellation were twinkling.

~

News awoke me… a storm, and before dawn I was stirred from slumber, urged to grab my sword.

"A riot!" one of Diego's servants said. "The Red Guards have stirred up the people."

It was Diego's actions that had stirred up the people… it was Diego who had driven the inhabitants of Asina Aurea into the

Red Guards' arms.

"You must help us! You must help us!"

I was not being paid. I had only been given a room, and food. But what else could I do but comply?

~

The people were desperate, and the motley group assembled had tears of anger in their eyes. They had gathered in the square outside Castle Ambra, and with sticks and knives and daggers, they were fighting vainly against the Zarube troops who now occupied their city. I was with the line of troops, under Diego's orders.

Among the mob were men with red scarves about their necks—the sign of the Red Guard. I tried to focus on them and not the people, them and not the desperate ones who'd had their nation taken from them.

With the pommel of my sword I beat at the rabble, not wishing to strike.

And from the crew assembled there was one I knew: Yacinda from The Crimson Cup, wielding a knife.

When she saw me her eyes watered and her lips trembled. She screamed at me, desperate, a wail—"Will you kill me Lorkdan, underworld's champion? Will you crush us all under your boot?"

Late in the day, the mob broke into its disparate parts, fleeing into the streets, and I did not pursue them. I felt dirty at what I had done, filthy even. I wanted to be gone from this land. I didn't know why I was staying here, why, so desperately, I sought the Briar Rose.

~

I returned to Castle Ambra. Before the spaciousness of Diego's throne room, I saw Elisette's petite form. There were bags in her hands, and bags slung over her shoulder. I drew near to her and said, under the breath, "Don't leave, not yet. Don't leave without me. The streets are not safe."

Chapter Twenty-Three: The Spark

Summer moved in; the heat grew. The situation in the city was quiet, but I sensed in my heart it was about to bubble over.

And on Midsummer's Day, in the warmth of one afternoon, that bad news arrived. The people were rising up… and they had help.

Part Seven

The Empire, the foreign nation I had first been conscripted to fight, had given help and aid to the rebels. Before their soldiers arrived, I whisked Elisette away, and riding on Lily we entered the Barrens' heat. I heard, on the road back to the Royal City, that Asina Aurea had quickly fallen, the knights and men-at-arms struck dead. Like his brother, Diego had been hanged from a tree.

And I had not found the Briar Rose.

—Lorkdan, "Records from Evre Prison"

Chapter Twenty-Four: Back Again

Past the Narrow Stream, the desert evaporated into lush forests, though now it was summer, and the air was dry, and no cloud could be seen drifting through the firmament.

I let Elisette ride on Lily, and throughout the day she would weep and cry out Diego's name. Her love was dead. And the nation we were entering was in more peril than ever before.

Elisette riding, I walking, we ventured northward up the road, past forests and villages and country inns, beside small towns that were growing larger and larger as the Royal City approached.

Peasants worked in country fields, and though the nation was in peril it seemed in better shape than I had left it. There was food at Ardogne's expense. Grain once again flowed, and when Elisette and I stopped to rest at public houses, the bread did not cost a *sou*, and the ale was cheap, though I felt I didn't much care for it now.

As for I and Elisette, I did not touch her, nor she me. She was like a delicate flower, and I had other things on my mind.

The road wound north under a blue sky. The summer crops were beginning to grow. And though war had been brought near, the faces in the fields and towns did not appear alarmed and worried, nor were they sickly and gaunt.

Many days after we had passed by the Narrow Stream, Elisette on Lily and I on foot passed over a hill, and below me appeared the staggering high walls of the Royal City, the stench of waste and tanneries detectable from where I stood. Yet other things were in the Royal City besides filth and squalor. There was life, there was vibrancy, there was opportunity. There was a life I had not forgotten, a promise I had made but failed to keep, a king, Bretagne, who I vowed to fight for but I had not.

I knew I walked into danger. But I would face danger like the man of war I was.

~

The streets were filled with people. The homes leaned so far they formed a tunnel. Carts filled with melons from Ardogne could be seen, and again the music from the public houses could be heard from the roadside.

But I had failed at what I sought to do. I had not found the woman Allórie's Briar Rose, if there was a briar rose to be found.

And Elisette was weeping, perhaps for a different reason, now.

"I am crying," Elisette said, "because I'm back home, where I belong… it has been so long. So many years—years that ended in tragedy."

"I think I know of a place you would enjoy," I told her.

I led her by the hand, through the filth-covered streets, down roads and through crowded market squares. I led her to the doors of The Belled Dancer, and on those doors I knocked.

~

The serving girl greeted me, and to my surprise there was a smile on her face.

"Lorkdan, underworld's champion," she said, "the master of this house has forgiven you your crimes. After all, it is said you are responsible for our good fortune… the grain supply."

It had not been my doing, but I saw why it might have been construed that way. I understood why in many tellings of a story, some might think that it was I, the translator and bodyguard that arranged the heist, and not the desperate King Diego.

"Welcome," she said, "again, Lorkdan, to The Belled Dancer. Your bed, and your ale, and your food will be free."

A strange thing, it was, to be provided something for free.

Chapter Twenty-Five: The Rose in Summer

I had a tall ale, no more than one.

Elisette had a small glass of wine, and she seemed uncomfortable at the sight of the dancing girls in brightly colored dresses, singing their chansons. It was not a place for a dignified woman like Elisette, and what's more, she had been apart from her homeland so long it surely seemed foreign to her.

As for me, the music enlivened my spirits, made me think my life was ahead of me, that possibilities were endless, that still there were foes to fight, and feats to accomplish.

The serving girl came by, asked if I wished for another ale.

"No," I told her, "no, thanks."

Her hair was dark, her eyes dark, too… and a feeling was planted in me, a strange desire that would lead me outside the tavern called The Belled Dancer.

"Will you go on a walk with me?" I said to Elisette.

Her wine glass was empty. She was in a city all alone. What could she do—say no?

~

Past piles of filth we walked, squalor, upturned carts, past wild animals, past painted prostitutes who apparently plied their trade even in the light of day. In the sun's warmth we walked, down damp alleys, through crowded streets, to a sumptuous manor with a metal gate, and beyond that gate a woman I knew—watering her rosebushes.

"Allórie! Allórie!'" I called out to her.

She stopped her watering and looked up.

The look that touched her eyes was first shock, then wonder, and then… then, she began to cry.

"Lorkdan," she said, "you have brought back the Briar Rose to me. You have brought back my Briar Rose!"

And I looked anew at Elisette, at her hair, a fiery red, at the fine gold gown she wore.

She had been the Briar Rose… this was what Allórie had desired—the Briar Rose, a woman, and not a rose forged of gold.

"Ah, Lorkdan, underworld's champion," said Allórie. "You are no vagabond like they say.

"And you may have more than *libres* and this house in the city… you may have all my wealth, all my holdings, everything… you, after all, have brought what I loved best to me.

"If she will stay with me."

"It had been a mistake to leave," Elisette said, and Allórie dropped her watering pail. She ran through the garden, to the gate, and opened it, still weeping.

She wrapped Elisette in her arms, in a tender embrace.

"I will give you everything, Lorkdan," the woman Allórie said to me. "Everything I have is yours…"

"No," I told Allórie. "No, no. I followed you for a feeling. Your words had planted that feeling in me. I will accept no reward; my reward is this sight."

Elisette began to weep, too, and then, hand in hand, Elisette and Allórie walked through the open gate to the doorway of Allórie's manse.

The sight warmed my heart, but the afternoon shadows were lengthening; the light of high noon cast all in an eerie illumination.

And I, feeling inexplicably vulnerable, hurried through the streets and alleyways toward the public house called The Belled

Dancer. My room and my meal were provided free.

What a strange thing it was to be provided something for free.

~

I had not made it to the door before a crowd overran me, knights in armor, some on horses, and in the distance a tall lanky figure I recognized, the shape of a lobster-like helm—Pago.

Others of his mercenaries stood behind him.

The king's punishment had at last come due.

Chapter Twenty-Six: The Figure in Light

The throne room of the Royal Castle was less splendid than that of Castle Ambra, and I wanted to say so.

The king called Bretagne sat in judgment on his throne, wearing over his body a robe of purple lined with white ermine. On his head was a bulky crown, on which were rows of ruby, sapphire and emerald. Bound about his neck was a gold necklace with a purple pendant. On his fingers were rings of gold, silver, and electrum.

Beside him in this place of judgment was Pago, the monster who had brutalized the villages of Aurange and Lys.

"He refused to carry out your judgment," said Pago. "Your judgment on the pretender."

Bretagne smiled. "That seems so unlike Lorkdan, the underworld's champion."

"He was just a boy!" I said.

"Can a boy not commit crimes?" Bretagne said. "A lapse in judgment… uncharacteristic. But it can be corrected."

He raised his right hand, and from a dark doorway came a number of more knights… and there… there among them…

I wanted to scream. The boy Jeoffre was there, not killed, left for me to do the dirty work, his hands bound in cord, his mouth muffled in cloth to hide any screams.

Jeoffre, Jeoffre… they demanded that I kill him. But I would not. I would not!

"I will not!" I shouted.

Jeoffre was resisting his binds. I would go to the dungeon, even to the notorious Evre Prison—but I would not spill the blood of that boy.

"I will not!" I said. "I will die first…"

But knights were behind me, and knights were in front of me. They seized me by the hands and twisted my arms behind my back. I resisted but there were too many.

"Perhaps," said King Bretagne, "you can be convinced."

He raised his left hand, and a servant walked out from a hidden doorway. In that servant's hand was a bowl, in that bowl white liquid.

The servant walked up to me, and I spat and I cursed. I resisted as mightily as I could, but there were too many of them, and only one of me.

To my lips the bowl was pressed, the milky white liquid, thick and bitter, and it trickled down my throat.

I staggered backward, freed from restraints. A light-wreathed figure appeared before me, and I knew in that instant his words were like the pronouncement of the gods, and what he said, I would do.

THE END

Glossary

Ardogne: A kingdom, built on a peninsula jutting southwestward from Zarubain. Winds and ocean effects create a dry, hot microclimate similar to those seen much farther south.

Asina Aurea: The capital of Ardogne, a massive metropolis containing most of the kingdom's population.

Badelgard: A small kingdom on a high plateau just north of Zarubain. Its warriors have been known to sail south and raid coastal towns.

Balzor: The god of the underworld and of death. Reverers of Balzor are considered strange and odd, and his worship is even banned in some kingdoms.

Berry Thicket: A small village in the nation of Gallia far east of Zarubain, located in the region of Estenmere.

Castle Ambra: A large castle in Asina Aurea, home to Ardogne's king, known for its crenelated towers and reddish stone.

County Neise: A county of the Eastern Heartlands.

County Valle: A county of the Eastern Heartlands. Its count was recently overthrown by a warrior named Lorkdan. The count has since been restored.

Duchy Lessant: A wealthy duchy on the west coast of Zarubain.

Evre Prison: A prison outside Zarubad, known for its poor treatment of prisoners. The worst criminals, including murderers and traitors, as well as prisoners of war, are held there.

Goddess, the: A term for Feanara, the goddess of the fey and woodland creatures, who is the patron deity of Zarubain.

Grieo: A general term, mostly pejorative, for the fairly-complected foreigners to Ardogne's east and north.

Lady's Cathedral, the: The largest cathedral in the world, dedicated to Zarubain's patron goddess, Feanara. It is the seat of the High Priestess and the site where kings of Zarubain are crowned.

Lion Throne, the: The throne of the King of Zarubain, located in the Royal Castle. It can also be the term for Zarubain in general.

Numinous Isles, the: Islands to the southwest of Ardogne, long considered sacred.

Red Guards, the: Originally street gangs that operated in the city of Asina Aurea, they have long called for the seizure of the wealth of the rich and the bourgeoisie and the redistribution of such funds to the poor. Historically, they were considered rebels to the Crown of Ardogne and driven underground, but the current king Jafet allied with them and empowered them, even allowing them to pilfer the wealth of Jafet's rich enemies and redistributing whatever coin and silver they seized as they saw fit.

River Garre: A long-flowing river of the Eastern Heartlands.

Royal City, the: A term for Zarubad.

St. Garroth: A fearsome warrior of olden days, the only saint in Balzor's religion, though most would say he did not act saintly. His symbols are the flail and the skull; lacquered black armor is the clothing of his devotees.

Toro: The patron god of Ardogne, represented as a bull.

Zarubad: The largest city of the Northern World, a metropolis, called the Royal City, located in the northwest of Zarubain.

Zarubain: A vast kingdom of the Northern World, stretching from the sea in the west to the nebulous border with Gallia to the east.

About the Author

Cursed at birth with a wild imagination, Andrew Cooper spent his youth dreaming of worlds more exciting than Earth.

He is a graduate of the Odyssey Writing Workshop. His stories have appeared in Morpheus Tales, Fear and Trembling, Residential Aliens and Mindflights, among others.

Contact the Author

Visit **www.aj-cooper.com** to sign up for the newsletter and stay up-to-date on new releases.

Find him on Facebook at:

www.facebook.com/AJCooperauthor

9 781958 724200